Ride A Summer Wind

Endorsements

With a story as captivating as its title, *Ride a Summer Wind* invites readers to step back in time to 1970's Spencer County, Indiana, where thirteen-year-old Buddie is caught up in an adventure involving the legacy of Abraham Lincoln. In this remarkable debut novel, Ann Cavera skillfully weaves together themes of friendship, forgiveness, and courage in this readable, relatable *and* educational tale.
—**Glenys Nellist**, award-winning children's author of 30+ titles including the Love Letters from God series and *I Wonder: Exploring God's Grand Story*

What a wonderful read! Ann Cavera proves a master at creating compelling characters and storylines in this can't-put-down mystery. *Ride a Summer Wind* may be aimed at middle-graders readers but will delight anyone who picks it up.
—**Caryn Rivadeneira**, award-winning author of the Frankinschool series

Ride a Summer Wind reads like a happy tune with the overtones of childhood joys and struggles. Ann Cavera's new book transports readers into the life of mandolin player Buddie, aka Apple Dumpling, and her precious

relationship with the grandfather who raised her. While the story takes the reader back decades, the themes of friendship and forgiveness, loss and love, are ever relevant and will be music to young hearts.
—**Amanda Cleary Eastep**, author of the Tree Street Kids series

Ann Cavera, author of *Ride a Summer Wind*, provides a wonderful new voice to the world of Christian Fiction for middle grade through young adult readers. Her words paint pictures of our world several decades ago, while touching the hearts of a contemporary audience burdened with coming-of-age concerns. The story rings with the sound of bluegrass music, family love and loss, and virtues left to the world by an admired historic figure, Abraham Lincoln. Humor lightens and enhances the story. *Ride a Summer Wind* offers hope, friendship, and forgiveness when the situation seems impossible. I highly recommend this author and book to all ages.
—**Bettie Boswell**, author of *Dottie's Dream Horse* and inspirational fiction for adults

Ann Cavera's beautiful novel reads like a relaxing canoe ride on a lake; easy, fun, exciting and inspirational. Her story is so very relatable to many ages lending itself to take you on a journey through love, family, friendship, forgiveness and human relationships! Cavera's story lovingly conveys that music is a part of the human soul connecting lives and experiences together. Enjoy every word of *Ride a Summer Wind*!
—**Traci Green** for The Hollow Trees, Family friendly music. Los Angeles, CA

Ride A Summer Wind

ANN CAVERA

Copyright Notice

Cover and Interior Design: Kelly Artieri, Deb Haggerty
Editor(s): Carol McClain, Cristel Phelps, Deb Haggerty

PUBLISHED BY: Elk Lake Publishing, Inc., 35 Dogwood Drive, Plymouth, MA 02360, 2024

Library Cataloging Data
Names: Cavera, Ann (Ann Cavera)
Ride a Summer Wind / Ann Cavera
188 p. 23cm × 15cm (9in × 6 in.)
ISBN-13: 9798891341647 (paperback) | 9798891341654 (trade paperback) | 9798891341661 (e-book)
Key Words: Middle-grade fiction; Grandparent-grandchild relationship; Mystery-stolen antiques; Faith and forgiveness; Bluegrass music; Family Relationships; Coming of Age
Library of Congress Control Number: 2024934017 Fiction

Dedication

Ride A Summer Wind is dedicated to the 2.5 million grandparents in the United States who provide love, energy, and resources to meet the needs of their grandchildren. Grandparents often have fixed incomes, and many struggle with health issues. With courage, they love and care for the children of their sons and daughters. These women and men are true unsung heroes.

Acknowledgments

With love and gratitude to my husband, Jim, and to our children and grandchildren. With love and gratitude to Gladys Williams Smith, my mother and my champion, my brother Mike, and our father, H. T. Smith.

I am ever grateful to my critique partner and friend, Bettie Boswell. You stand steadfast with words of wisdom and encouragement. Thanks to Sue A. Fairchild who helped prepare the story for submission. With gratitude to Deb Haggerty, Cristel Phelps, Carol McClain, and Kelly Artieri at Elk Lake Publishing for patience, understanding, and grace to know creativity matures but does not age.

Thanks to Cynthia Leitich-Smith. Your words, “Never doubt that you have a seat at this table,” gave me hope for the journey. With gratitude to Brian Allain for much encouragement along the way. Also, with gratitude to Madeleine L’Engle who, long ago, helped me believe.

Chapter 1

The Vase on the Shelf

The final bell clanged. Lockers slammed for the last time, and school doors flew open. I bolted outside with the rest of the eighth grade. That's the way the summer of 1977 began in Whistler, Indiana.

"Buddie! Buddie!" Wait up!"

I looked straight ahead, pretending not to hear Keach calling my name. All she ever talked about was how we were going to win first place in the talent show. Why did I ever agree to play my mandolin with her in front of the whole town?

"Be sure and wear dark red lipstick. Don't forget to bow when we win." If I heard those words one more time, I'd throw her banjo and my mandolin on the ground and stomp them to bits right before her eyes.

"Apple Dumpling!" Keach screamed. A few kids around me snickered when they heard my real name. My mama was a flower child back in the sixties. Grandpa said flower children liked to give their babies memorable names. I remember Mama handing me to Grandpa on his front porch when I was six years old.

"Hi, Daddy," she said. "See? I brought you a grandbaby."

Grandpa hugged me, looked into my eyes and smiled. "She's cute as a doodlebug. I'm so glad you've come home. Let's go inside."

"Can't stay, Daddy, but I need you to watch her for a few days. Her name is Apple Dumpling." Mama skipped down the porch steps and ran back to her car.

Grandpa shouted after her. "Apple Dumpling? Apple Dumpling? What kind of name is that for a child?" Without another word, Mama sped away. Much to my everlasting relief, Grandpa always called me Buddie.

Keach fell into step beside me. "We need to walk home together and go over the plan for tonight."

"I am done talking about the talent show. If you promise not to say another word about how I'm supposed to act on stage, we'll walk together. If you start up, I'm running home. You can follow me hollering Apple Dumpling all you want. I'm never stopping."

"Maybe we can talk about how we can get Adam to like you instead of Courtney."

"No. I don't want to talk about Adam, either.

"Can we talk about the vase? Did Mrs. Nelson like the color?"

Mrs. Nelson helped me so much with my writing I wanted to give her a gift at the end of the school year. Keach knew I planned to give my teacher a crimson glass vase from Grandpa's kitchen shelf. After all, how important could an old vase full of our unpaid bills be?

"Yes. I polished Grandpa's vase, and went straight to her classroom before the bell rang this morning. She said my crimson vase is the prettiest one she has ever seen, and teaching me has been a pleasure."

"What did Lutie say when you asked him about giving her the vase?"

I didn't answer Keach right away. Cars passed by with horns blaring celebrating the last day of school. "I didn't ask. Grandpa went into the woods before I woke up. He won't mind me giving away a piece of junk."

Grandpa and I lived in a little frame house with a tin roof beyond the edge of town. His real name was Luther Ethan McBride, and he was a luthier. A luthier makes stringed instruments. Most people called him Lutie for short. People often said Grandpa made the most beautiful mandolins and banjos in the Indiana hill country.

Keach and I stopped at the edge of my yard. "Don't be late tonight. I'm going extra early. I'll be there waiting for you." She ran toward her house a quarter mile down the road.

Grandpa waited for me on the front porch. Instead of his usual friendly wave, he stomped back and forth so hard the floorboards rattled beneath his boots. As soon as he saw me, he yelled, "Where's my vase?"

"That old thing? I ... I needed a gift for Mrs. Nelson. She was my best teacher ever. You were in the woods." My words sounded fuzzy when I tried to explain.

"You have no idea what you've done." Fierce anger made the veins on his neck stand out. "I can't talk to you about this right now." He stormed inside, slammed the screen door, and cooked supper without another word.

When we sat down to eat, the wrinkles in his forehead pinched his bushy white brows together over his nose. After a quick, mumbled "Bless us, O Lord ..." he hunched over his plate and ate in silence. I shoveled down my beans and cornbread, thinking I'd stay quiet while he sorted his thoughts. Though grateful he didn't want to talk, I worried about why the vase mattered.

After supper, Grandpa dropped his dishes in the sink. "Let's sit on the front porch for a bit."

I thought he might want to talk about the vase while we sat outside. Instead, we quietly watched the sun tint wispy clouds summer shades of pink and orange. Troublesome as his silence felt, dread of standing on stage that night edged out my shame over taking his vase.

I tried to make a joke. "Grandpa, I don't want to go to the talent show. I have decided to nail my shoes to this porch." With a quick sideways glance, I saw he was not smiling.

His rocking chair creaked to a stop. "Buddie, I've told you before, the joy you have in music won't spread unless you give it away. Besides, Keach can't pick her banjo well enough to stand up there by herself, and I did not raise you to go back on your word."

If my dumbest decision, ever, was taking Grandpa's vase without asking, the second dumbest decision had to be agreeing to play in the Spencer County Talent Contest. I searched my brain for a rock-solid reason not to leave the sweet safety of our porch. With no way out of the show, I sighed, went inside, and changed into my stage outfit. A few minutes later, I grabbed my mandolin and came outside ready to leave.

Grandpa pinched a couple of mint leaves growing in a pot next to his rocker and stuffed them in his mouth. He snacked on plants the way other people ate potato chips and pretzels. Mint and parsley sweetened breath. Garlic stopped chest pains. He called plants "God's pharmacy."

Grandpa pushed himself out of his chair and eased down the steps. I hitched up my skirt and followed him. I'd go to the talent show. I'd stand on stage and make a fool of myself. After all, I owed him that much for taking his vase without asking.

There we were, with me now thirteen-years-old, shuffling down the road past a billowing honeysuckle vine weighing down a cattle fence. I reached into the vine and picked one of the trumpet-shaped blossoms. A startled monarch butterfly danced above the mass of yellow flowers. Breathing in the heavy honeysuckle scent, I bit off the narrow end of the blossom, and sucked out a sweet drop of nectar.

Half an hour later, we arrived at Spencer County High. That's where my worst fear of hundreds of ears listening for me to pick a wrong note was about to come true. The outside of the metal stage door bore a huge dent over the handle. Performers often pounded on this door to get somebody to let them in. Tonight, the door stood propped open. Warm air and voices filtered outside. Grandpa's face softened into a wistful smile. He put his arm around my shoulders. "Buddie, I love you. You're worth more than all the vases in this world."

I nearly cried with relief. "Thanks, Gramps. Next time, I'll ask before I take anything."

With a gentle hug and nudge, he sent me from the peace and quiet of the countryside into a backstage world of noise and lights.

Chapter Two

Backstage Jitters

Inside the door, six steps led up to the stage area where performers milled. Dozens of feet mixed the scent of paste wax on old wood floors with the smell of fresh poster paint. On the opposite side of the stage, a break in the curtains led to a backstage waiting area for performers. Behind the waiting area, a door opened to a short flight of stairs going down into the auditorium.

In the backstage confusion, I had no idea where to go until I spotted Keach sitting on a stool at the far end of the closed stage curtain.

She fidgeted with the ropes and pulleys used for opening the curtains. As soon as she saw me, a sizable smile of relief crossed her face.

I sat on a stool next to her. "You know I don't want to be here."

"Glad you decided to show up." Keach fingered her banjo and strummed a chord. "I thought me and my banjo might have to win this contest all by ourselves. Anyway, you're here now, and there's no backing out. This will be easy cash for both of us. You'll thank me once we're rich and famous."

"That's how you see things. All you think about is money, which mostly doesn't matter to me. You can thank Grandpa you're not sitting here alone."

"So, you'll settle for being stuck right here in Whistler, Indiana, forever? Maybe you're afraid Adam will be upset when we take first prize away from him?" A sly smile crossed her face.

"Adam's my friend. That's all." I shrugged as if I didn't care.

Adam's family owned a big farm down the road from our place. We grew up running around in the woods together. I watched his uncle from Albuquerque teach him how to play classical guitar while everybody else in southern Indiana played fiddles, mandolins, and banjos. Last summer, Adam started spending all his free time with Courtney Castleberry. After that, he didn't have time to be friends with me or anybody else.

"You might try flirting a little. See? Like this." Keach raised her chin and winked.

"Adam would laugh if I did that. Besides, what am I supposed to do about Courtney? Walk up and say, 'Excuse me. I'm here to flirt with your boyfriend?'"

At that moment, Courtney hurried past with Adam close behind her. She pushed aside a couple of costumes on a bench to make room for her red, fake-alligator-hide makeup case. With a quick dance step, she whirled, faced Adam, and smoothed the collar on his dark green plaid shirt. He smiled his crooked half-smile like he always did when he got nervous. Glancing my way, he nodded and then told Courtney he had to change a guitar string.

Courtney opened her mouth to speak, but then she stopped and turned at the sound of high heels click-clacking across the stage. "Ma, you're not supposed to be back here!"

"Nonsense, darlin'." Cee Cee Castleberry smoothed her daughter's hair. "That doesn't apply to parents."

Grandpa might have said Cee Cee's jeans looked painted on. An ankle bracelet glittered above her silver high heels.

Cee-Cee leaned over and patted Courtney's hair. "You can do this baby, you can do this," Cee Cee crooned, lifting Courtney's chin. With an index finger on each of Courtney's cheeks, she pulled her daughter's mouth into a mirthless grin. "Smile, baby, always smile. Now you just relax. Remember, keep your head high, shoulders straight, and *have a good time*. Don't worry, and don't you forget to put in the fancy little step you learned last week. Ain't this fun?"

Giving Courtney's hair a final pat, Cee Cee scurried away like a starving mouse in search of a golden crumb. Courtney slumped on the bench and buried her face in her hands.

Having her mom always hanging around had to be hard for Courtney. Still, I wished I had a mom wanting to spend time with me.

"Look, Keach. See the way light sparkles off those blue sequins on Courtney's costume? She'll dance away with first prize."

"Your eyes sparkle more than those sequins, and she's too short for Adam. Bet he'd have to squat to kiss her, which I hope you noticed he did not do."

Courtney dropped a lipstick, stood, and stepped on the tube to stop it from rolling. She bent over and snatched the lipstick from the floor.

Keach giggled. "Look at the size of the hole in the back of Miss Perfect's pantyhose."

Sure enough, a rip the size of a quarter gaped in the back of one of Courtney's black net stockings.

The hole in Courtney's stocking made me worry about how I looked. Keach and I had spent several days hand-sewing our outfits. I ran my hand over the waistband of my long, red-gingham skirt. "Are you sure this is the way Loretta Lynn makes her skirts?

"I'm sure. I saw her sew one on a TV show exactly like I showed you. She took a long piece of cloth for the waistband. Then she stitched a bunch of material inside the band to make a skirt. Works fine. See?" Keach reached out and gave my waistband a yank.

"Keep your hands to yourself. If our skirts fall off in public, we'll be famous long before we get rich." I turned away and peeked through a hole in the curtain in time to see Grandpa take an aisle seat near the back of the auditorium. Did he truly forgive me for the vase?

Chapter Three

The Vase Reappears

Keach and I both wore white blouses, but she had replaced a missing button on her blouse with a green rhinestone four-leaf-clover pin. I'd watched her pay twenty-five cents for the pin at a church rummage sale.

Keach flashed her cockiest grin. "I need first prize to get away from here."

"That's only fifty dollars for each of us. Remember what happened the last time you ran off with no money?"

Keach winced. "I'll never let Pa catch me sitting on my suitcase beside the highway again." Beneath her breath she added, "Next time, I'll have a perfect plan."

"I wish you'd stop talking about sneaking off. I want to see how people live in exotic places like Spain, France, and even Chicago as much as you do. We'll leave after high school."

"Maybe I'll wait. Last week, Pa went to an auction in Lexington. Two weeks ago, he spent three days in St. Louis. I'm already next to a cat's breath of living alone."

I pulled the edge of the curtain back an inch and pointed to her father making his way to the last vacant seat in the front row. "Look, he's here tonight."

Keach pushed me aside to see for herself. A cold, faraway look settled in her face. The auburn bangs she had trimmed hung in ragged clumps above her hazel eyes. Her mouth tightened in a hard line and stayed that way until the call came for performers to gather for final instructions.

My history teacher, Miss Emily, motioned for quiet. She wasn't an inch over five feet tall. With her silver hair cut in a stylish pixie, and her wire-rimmed granny glasses, she appeared to be a woman who meant business. Still teaching eighth graders after forty years, she kept her energy level charged and her eyes and mind open.

Miss Emily raised her hand, and everyone stopped talking. "We're about to turn up the stage lights and raise the curtain. When I announce your act, people will applaud. Come to center stage. Wait for the applause to stop before you begin. Bow at the end while people are applauding and leave the stage. Go through the backstage door into the auditorium. Sit in the seats on the front right-hand side reserved for performers who have competed. Any questions?"

Butch Weems raised his hand. "Can performers have some of the cookies afterwards?" Tall, thin, and athletic, Butch Weems had a perpetual, consuming interest in food.

Miss Emily nodded. "Yes, but don't take more than two or three. We have a lot of people here tonight."

The house lights dimmed, and we waited for the audience to settle into seats. Miss Emily left for a few minutes. When she returned, her arms were full of early summer pink roses. She stopped in front of me. "Buddie, one of the parents brought these for the refreshment table. Did I hear you gave Mrs. Nelson a vase today?"

"Yes, a red one about a foot high."

"I'll check with her during intermission."

I watched Miss Emily hurry off while the fragile scent of roses lingered in the air. My stomach tightened. Would Grandpa be upset all over again if he saw his vase on the refreshment table?

"Look at you." Keach interrupted my thoughts. "Why are you standing here with your face all red?"

"When I got home this afternoon, Grandpa was upset about the vase. That's all."

"Old people get attached to weird stuff." Courtney stood nearby. She obviously heard every word we said.

Keach clenched her teeth and got right in Courtney's face. "Mind your own business."

Courtney gave Keach a quick shove and made her fall against me. "I'm not interested in anything the two of *you* have to say. I've been trying to tell both of you to move back. This is my place in line." She squeezed in front of us.

A minute or two later Miss Emily returned, checked the lineup, and walked onstage to announce the first act. As she called one name after another, my palms grew sweaty.

Right before Miss Emily announced Courtney Castleberry, Keach tapped her on the shoulder. "You might like to know, there's a big hole in the back of one of your stockings."

Courtney gave Keach a venomous stare. "This is a brand-new pair. They cost ten dollars."

Since Keach delivered her news with a look of pure, shocked innocence, Courtney twisted her head down and back, searching for the rip.

"Right here," Keach snagged a finger in the rip. The hole popped wider.

Miss Emily announced, "Next, Courtney Castleberry will dance to 'Ain't She Sweet.'"

Courtney sneered at Keach. "Little people notice small things." She tapped her way on stage without turning her back to the audience.

Courtney's mom sat in the middle of the front row with her fingers pulling at each corner of her mouth, silently reminding Courtney to smile.

"Keach, that was mean. You tried to spook her on purpose."

"Maybe, but nothing I say will make any difference. I hear her mama has been hauling her over to Louisville for dance lessons since she was two. Courtney's problem is she has no talent. She won't beat us tonight. Nobody will."

At the end of Courtney's performance, she flounced offstage.

Keach snorted and made a face.

As Courtney walked past us, she paused to stomp on Keach's toes.

"Next chance I get, I'll trip her." Keach said, making a face behind Courtney's back.

"Don't bother." I ran my fingers across my mandolin strings. "Here," I reached for her banjo. "Let me help you tune up. As soon as intermission is over, we're on."

Chapter Four

Curious Questions

During intermission, Miss Emily left the stage area. A few minutes later, she returned with the pink roses in a very familiar vase. “Buddie, aren’t these roses perfect in your vase?” Miss Emily held the vase and bouquet in front of my face. The pale roses appeared to have pinched a bit of crimson from the vase and transformed the color into the pink light of dawn. The beautiful combination took my breath away.

Miss Emily hurried off toward the door separating the backstage area from the auditorium. As she reached for the doorknob, she stopped, raised the vase to her eye level, and examined the crimson glass carefully. Drops of water from the rose leaves fell on her black dress. With a puzzled look, she went through the doorway and down into the auditorium.

I peeked around the edge of the curtain and watched as she studied the refreshment table below the stage. After talking about how pretty the vase and flowers were, why did she nearly hide the whole arrangement behind a pitcher of lemonade?

The house lights dimmed, signaling the end of intermission. A hush fell over the audience. Miss Emily announced, "Buddie McBride and Katherine 'Keach' Webb with a rendition of "Pretty Polly.""

Keach pulled me from behind the curtain. The audience spun in a blur. Thankfully, the stage lights kept me from seeing individual faces beyond the first two rows.

This is for you, Grandpa. From the moment I hit the first notes, music rolled easily from beneath my fingers. I imagined Grandpa's smile breaking across the wrinkles on his face. I thought I saw a couple of farmers drumming fingers against the knees of clean work jeans. Was that a young mother in the second row bouncing her baby to the rhythm of our picking? Worrisome thoughts about the vase, Courtney, and gaps in Keach's timing faded as my heart flew wild and free riding the old-time rhythm. With a little shock, I realized speaking my heart with music came easier than putting thoughts into words.

We bowed as soon as we finished and left the stage with applause ringing in our ears. Keach grinned and whispered, "Didn't I tell you? We'll flat-out win this thing."

"I'm not seeing any money in my hand yet, but at least our skirts didn't fall off. Maybe you're right. We might not go home empty-handed."

We crossed the backstage area and went down the steps into the auditorium. Six acts came after us. From our seats in the auditorium, we clapped politely for each act following ours. When Miss Emily announced Adam as the final act, I applauded extra hard. The rich chords pouring from beneath Adam's fingers made me think of Spain with silver-spurred riders in fancy saddles on galloping horses. I remembered seeing pictures of such riders in the dusty *National Geographic* magazines Grandpa kept stacked beneath our beds.

After Adam's solo, the audience murmured while the judges tallied their votes. Miss Emily called all the contestants back onstage for a round of applause. Finally, she stepped forward. “Ladies and Gentlemen—” At that moment the microphone emitted a skin-crawling screech. She took a step back. “I am happy to announce the winners of the 1977 Spencer County Indiana Talent Contest.”

The audience grew quiet anticipating the results.

I too held my breath, wondering what would come next.

Keach grasped my shoulder as we leaned forward to hear the news.

We breathed easier when the twenty-five-dollar third prize went to a flute soloist. “One down, one more before we start to get rich,” Keach whispered.

When the flute player stepped to the front of the stage, her daddy stood up and yelled, “Whoo-hoo! Baby girl! Whoo-hoo!” The winner smiled, but her face turned red. She grabbed her prize money, made a quick bow, and ran back to join the rest of us.

Miss Emily returned to the microphone. “Second prize of fifty dollars goes to Buddie McBride and Katherine ‘Keach’ Webb for their lively version of ‘“Pretty Polly.’”

Keach pushed me out in front of her. I stumbled a little, and a kid in the audience snickered. That night, I realized it is not always easy to act happy about second place. Adam collected the hundred-dollar first prize, and I forced myself to smile and congratulate him. With Courtney jumping up and down hugging him so hard, I doubt he heard me.

Keach shook her head. “The way Courtney acts, you’d think she won first prize.”

“It sure looks that way.” I held out Keach’s half of our cash.

She crumpled her twenty and a five into a wad. “This ain’t worth spit.”

I folded my money and rubbed the bills between my fingers. "I've got more than enough to buy a couple of things I want."

Performers wandered off in different directions. People in the audience streamed toward the refreshment table below the stage.

"Let's get down into the auditorium. I need to find Grandpa."

We joined the crowd around the refreshment table, but Grandpa wasn't there.

Keach smoothed her twenty-dollar bill and her five-dollar bill and wove them in and out of her banjo strings. "Here comes my pa, looking for food. He'll stuff his face with punch and cookies before he bothers finding me."

Mr. Webb ignored the cookies. He reached behind the pitcher of lemonade and ran his hand over the crimson vase. "I wonder who brought these beautiful roses?" His raspy voice carried above the murmur of the crowd, but no one seemed to notice.

At that moment, Miss Emily tapped me on the shoulder. "Buddie?" She zapped me with her "don't move" look, and I froze in place. "Mrs. Nelson says she thinks Lutie may have owned his vase for a long time. Did he ever mention the history?"

"I ... I don't know. That vase has been in our kitchen ever since my mama ..." *Would Miss Emily or Mrs. Nelson guess I couldn't afford to buy a gift? Even worse, would either of them think I picked up a piece of junk at a yard sale just to have a present for my teacher?*

"I need to speak to Lutie," Miss Emily glanced around the room.

I gulped. "He's here tonight."

"Do you still play music on your porch after supper?"

What was she getting at? "Yes, ma'am. If the evening turns rainy or cold, I practice inside."

"Tell Lutie I'll stop by after supper in a day or two."

Keach watched Miss Emily leave, and then she turned to me. "Why are people asking questions about Lutie's vase?"

I shrugged and looked out over the crowd, hoping to see Grandpa.

As Keach reached for a handful of cookies, her father grabbed her shoulder, and he shook my hand. "Nice work, Buddie. Thanks for teaching Katherine how to play. I'm glad she's got a good friend." He smiled a tobacco-stained smile, and then added softly, "I'm sorry, Katherine, but we need to go now. I've got to get up early tomorrow."

"Can't I stay here a while with Buddie?"

I stared down at the yellow daisies Grandpa carved and painted on the back of my mandolin. Sweat made my blouse stick to my shoulder blades.

"Not tonight." As Mr. Webb steered Keach toward the outside door, he looked back at me. "Better luck next time on first place."

Keach glanced back with a look of defeat. As soon as they left, I searched the crowd, trying to find Grandpa. People kept stopping me and saying things like "Nice work. You've got your grandpa's hands." Finally, I found him talking to neighbors at the back of the auditorium. After giving him a hug, I held up my twenty and five. "Now I'll buy you a new shirt."

He threw a bony arm across my shoulders. "The way you played made a better present than money can buy. Congratulations! You deserved a prize."

So glad he was pleased, I beamed. "Music isn't a real present. I'll buy you a blue shirt to match your eyes."

Grandpa shook his head. "There's no better gift than music. Besides, I've already got three shirts. You need to spend a few dollars on that Bill Monroe album you saw in Emily's Attic."

On weekends and during summer vacations, Miss Emily ran an antique store from the first floor of her house on Main Street. In addition to antiques, she sold stationery, tapes, and records. I spent plenty of hot summer afternoons hanging out in her store, listening to old music, and soaking up the free air conditioning.

"What about other things we need like getting the lock fixed on the back door?"

"Don't worry about the lock. We'll never have everything we need. Now and then, we ought to enjoy whatever we want. Buy the record and let Keach listen to the music. Maybe she'll learn to play a few more songs. We'll fix the lock on the back door as soon as we win the sweepstakes."

"That's right. I forgot." I always teased him when he talked about how we were going to win the *Reader's Digest* sweepstakes any day and never be short of cash again. That night, I went along with him. I wanted to get him out of the auditorium before he noticed the vase. "What about an ice cream cone to eat on the way home? My treat now that I'm rich."

Grandpa smiled. "Lots of folks will be stopping for ice cream. Can I have my favorite?"

Dancing backward a few steps in front of him, I said, "Well Gramps, we'd better hurry or there won't be any Rocky Road left." Tomorrow, I'd tell him how curious Miss Emily had been about his vase. Nothing that evening would spoil the feeling of my mandolin slung across my back and cash in my hand.

Chapter Five

An Idea for Keach

Saturday morning, I skipped breakfast and took a shortcut through the woods to Keach's house. I wanted her to pay for half of the Bill Monroe album at Miss Emily's shop before she blew her prize money. Keach talked a lot about saving, but cash slipped through her fingers as fast as a wet fish off a hook. A warm breeze played with new green leaves overhanging the path while my tennis shoes kicked up puffs of dry dirt. I kept hoping Mr. Webb would be gone when I got to their place.

Nobody knew much about Keach or her dad. They'd moved to Whistler a year earlier, and Mr. Webb worked in different cities as an auctioneer. According to Keach, they came to Whistler to get a fresh start after her mother died. The sound of my music drew her to our porch.

When we first met Keach, her sadness reminded me how I felt right after my mom left me with Grandpa. Mom promised she would come back for me soon, but all we ever got were a few postcards. Even those stopped after a couple of years. Music eased my lonesome feelings, and Grandpa thought music might do the same for Keach. A banjo is easier to play than a mandolin, so we gave her a banjo and taught her to play. Soon, she spent most of her free time at our house.

When Mr. Webb's black pickup truck came into view at the far end of the path, I slowed to a walk. He and Keach lived in a shotgun style house with a front and back porch like ours—neat and tidy from the outside. Not many people knew Mr. Webb crammed every room with antiques he brought home from auctions. He liked to keep to himself.

Beyond the screen door, the front door stood open. The drawn window shades kept the living room dark. As I walked across the porch, a musty smell seeped out through the screen door. The voices of two men came from the kitchen in the rear of the house.

Keach answered when I knocked, but she stayed inside the screen door.

I asked, "Who's here?"

"Clem Farney. He's going to help Pa move furniture at an auction. He says being a part-time school janitor don't pay beans."

"He's a drifter. I don't know why Principal Reed hired him." I looked over her shoulder into the dim interior of the house, hoping Clem didn't hear me.

Keach chuckled. "Some of the older boys like him. They skip classes to take a smoke with him in the furnace room. He tells them exciting stories about his adventures as a traveling bum. Don't worry, Clem's harmless."

"Maybe, but he won't do anybody much good either."

"Girl!" Mr. Webb called from the kitchen. "Where's our coffee?"

"One of these days, I'm going to give him his coffee right in his face." Keach unlatched the screen door, and I followed her down the hall.

Mr. Webb nodded when he saw me. He didn't invite me to sit down, so I leaned against the kitchen doorway. Keach filled the empty cups on the table in front of Clem and her father. As she worked, quiet covered the room like a layer of moss. The splashing of coffee in the cups and the ticking of a mantel clock in an open cupboard breathed life into the silence.

Mr. Webb grasped his cup in both hands and peered inside. "Buddie, did those roses on the refreshment table last night come from Lutie's garden?"

"No."

"Oh. My mistake. I thought I heard Mrs. Nelson say those came from you."

"Only the vase." I crossed my arms over my waist. "Grandpa used that old vase for holding unpaid bills." I shifted my weight against the doorframe and regretted mentioning our unpaid bills.

"Unpaid bills? Unpaid bills!" Mr. Webb chuckled in a way that sent coffee rippling over the rim of his cup. "You're right. The vase is old and might have brought a few bucks at an auction. Tell Lutie if he's got any other antiques, I'll gladly auction them off for him before you go giving everything away. I might even get enough to clear up your unpaid bills."

With a few loud gulps, Mr. Webb drained his cup. I caught a glimpse of Keach looking over at me. Her eyes narrowed, and she shook her head.

Clem leaned back in his chair. "Speaking of unpaid bills, them's exactly what I'm hoping to clear up for myself with this extra work."

"What you get from me depends on how much you're able to do," Mr. Webb told him. "If we don't get going, you won't make enough to even buy beans."

"'Course, with my back problem, I can't lift too much." Clem guzzled the last of his coffee, wiped his mouth on his sleeve, and eased out of his chair.

"Humph! If you can't do what I ask, I'll hire me somebody able to work." Mr. Webb herded Clem out the door and into the truck.

As soon as they drove away, Keach dropped four slices of bread into the toaster, and we sat at the round oak table. When the toast popped up, she opened a drawer and pulled out an antique silver knife with a likeness of one of the presidents molded on the handle. She held the knife in front of her face. "Good morning, George Washington." Keach smeared all four pieces of toast with crunchy peanut butter. She always made peanut butter toast for breakfast because, except for the knife, there would be no dishes to wash.

"Why did you look at me when your dad asked about the vase?" I asked as she put two of the slices in front of me on the table.

"Pa's a sharp businessman. The main person he's interested in helping is himself. Didn't want you to think he'd be looking to do you any favors." She bit into one of her pieces of toast and chewed.

A few minutes later, I finished my toast and licked the last of the peanut butter off my fingers. "Speaking of doing us a favor—" I imitated Clem's high, squeaky voice—"that's why I'm here. Miss Emily has a Bill Monroe album we can buy and use to learn more songs."

"I need to save every penny I've got." Keach brushed an ant from the tabletop.

"If we split the cost, we'll both still have money. You can save yours. I'll buy a shirt for Grandpa. After you study the songs, learning a couple of new pieces will be easy."

"If listening will help me learn to play new tunes, then I'd call that a wise investment," Keach imitated her father's hoarse voice. "An investment isn't like spending money at all. Let me change my shirt, and we'll go into town and take a look."

Chapter Six

Strange Encounters

As we walked into town, the smell of fertilizer blew across the corn and soybean fields on either side of the road. I pointed at two crows circling above us, cawing back and forth. "Sounds like they're having a conversation. What do you think they're saying?"

"That's easy. One bird is asking, 'Who are those two girls down there?' The other one replies, 'Don't you know? There goes the world-famous bluegrass duo of Webb and McBride.'"

"McBride and Webb," I corrected her. My stomach growled. I wished I had eaten more than two slices of toast.

A gold-painted Volkswagen Beetle roared past, kicking up a fine layer of dust and straw. The driver sat hunched over with his sharp chin nearly pressing the steering wheel. A shorter, heavier man occupied the passenger's seat. As they swerved around us, the passenger tossed a piece of paper out of his window. Keach picked up the paper. "Ewwww! This is a sticky Butterfinger wrapper."

"Serves you right. See what you get for picking up other people's trash?" I laughed as she tried to deal with the messy paper.

Keach folded the wrapper around a pebble and threw the rock at a sign welcoming people to Whistler, Indiana, Pop. 6,000. "You never know. What if we didn't bother to look? We might walk right past a prize-winning golden ticket. Pa says we've got to seize our opportunities."

The VW disappeared around a bend in the road where two horseback riders pulled their mounts aside to let the car pass.

"Look," Keach pointed to the riders. "There's Adam, still following Courtney. "Thinking in terms of opportunities, this might be one for you."

"Courtney won't bother speaking to us, and Adam won't stop if she doesn't." I squinted in their direction.

"This is your chance," Keach said. "If you can't speak up, I will. After I start talking, you ask him a question about where they've been. That'll be easy enough."

I opened my mouth to tell Keach to keep hers shut, but by then Adam and Courtney were too close. My palms were wet, and the space inside my head where my brain usually worked turned into warm butterscotch pudding. Courtney barely nodded when she passed. Adam halted his horse, but he stayed in the saddle.

Keach smiled at him. "You did a nice job last night."

"The two of you were tough competition." He glanced down the road to where Courtney waited. "Maybe we could play together sometime."

Before I answered, Keach blurted, "We won't play anywhere unless we get paid."

I stared at her with my mouth open. Of course, we wanted to earn money with our music, but how could she throw away Adam's generous offer to practice?

"That true, Buddie?" He turned my way and appeared to study my face. "These days you play only for money?"

Working in the fields left Adam's face and arms with a deep tan. Farm work ripped holes in his jeans.

I rubbed my hand across small beads of foam on his mare's dark neck. More than anything, I wanted to tell Adam how much my music meant to me, but the best I managed was, "I'll always play, whether anybody pays or even listens."

He smiled. "I know what you mean. I'm the same way about my guitar."

"You and Courtney coming from town?" Keach asked.

"We've been working on the 4-H project helping restore the old Lincoln homestead on the other side of town. Tourists will be able to see how the farm looked when Abe lived there a hundred and fifty years ago." Adam paused then added, "We need more help. Want to give us a hand?"

Keach shook her head. "That sounds like a lot of hard work."

Courtney jerked her horse's bridle and called, "Hurry up, Adam. I need to get home."

"Lincoln's farm is an interesting place." Adam nudged his horse and turned to leave.

"Adam, wait!" I shouted and ran to catch up to him. "I want to help."

Adam stared at the top of my head for a moment before replying. "Great. Come by after lunch any day during the week." Pointing to the top of my head, Adam leaned from his saddle and plucked a single piece of straw from my hair. "This is the same color as your hair." He slipped the golden straw between his teeth, grinned, and rode away.

I went back to where Keach waited. "Not only did I talk to Adam, but we're going to meet at the Lincoln farm one afternoon, no thanks to you." I walked by her, feeling a bit smug.

Keach caught up with me. "Let me remind you who started that conversation. Next time, you can break the ice all by yourself."

"Promise?" I scowled at her. "And what did you mean about us getting paid to play? Nobody around here is going to hire us."

"Not around here. We might have to leave to find work."

Keach liked to talk about leaving Whistler. "When I go," I reminded her, "I want people standing around and wishing me luck. I won't be sneaking out in the middle of the night, begging a ride from any stranger passing through town."

Keach looked away from me into the distance. "Even if you stay here forever, you'll never be able to count on Adam. Courtney pulls him around the same way she yanks the bridle on that horse of hers."

"Who's worried about Adam?" Fanning a bug away from my face, I caught the scent of Adam's mare lingering on my fingers. I turned back in time to catch a glimpse of the horses and riders disappearing around the bend.

Keach tapped me on the shoulder. "If we're ever going to get out of town, planning for a far-off perfect day to leave won't work. All great people know how to seize the moment. That's how they get to be great. When my moment comes, I'm leaving." She made a quick fist with her hand as if yanking a fleeting chance out of midair. "Your problem is you don't know how to take things for yourself."

I remembered the way Adam smiled and took the straw from my hair. "You might be wrong about that. I think maybe I just did."

By the time we reached Emily's Attic, I had almost stopped thinking about Adam. On the long wide porch beside the etched glass front door, Miss Emily displayed a poster advertising the Bluegrass Music Festival in Bean Blossom, Indiana. Every summer, Grandpa and I hitched a ride two hours north to the festival where we sold any instruments we'd finished. Those trips were about as close as we ever came to a real vacation.

Inside Emily's Attic, sturdy oak tables overflowed with carnival glass dishes and stacks of tattered books smelling of dusty closets in old houses. We made our way between rows of open cupboards filled with salt and pepper shakers, cast iron banks, and doll-sized porcelain tea sets.

Miss Emily straightened up from a crate she had been unpacking. "I saved this for you." She handed me Bill Monroe's *Blue Grass Special* album from 1963.

We sprawled on the floor beside a record player plugged into an outlet and listened to Bill Monroe pick a mandolin in ways I could only dream. At the end of the first side, the sleigh bells attached to the front door jangled. In barged the two men from the Volkswagen on the highway.

"Hullo? Anybody here?" The hawk-faced man from the driver's seat edged his way between the tables. His companion pushed in behind him, nearly knocking over a painted ceramic umbrella stand beside the door.

"Can I help you fellows?" Miss Emily asked.

The tall man spread a map across the counter. "I'm Claude Stone and this is my partner, Wilbur Waters. We're surveyors, ma'am, sent to update maps for this area. The motel owner told us you might pinpoint recent changes in the back roads."

"Surveyors, are you?" Miss Emily raised her eyebrows.

Wilbur slid a couple of steps backward. "We certainly are." He fished his wallet from his pocket. A mint stuck to the leather. He popped the candy into his mouth and flashed an official-looking card. "Here's proof." Before

Miss Emily managed to read the small print on the card, Wilbur jammed both the card and wallet back in his hip pocket.

Claude bent over the map. "Ma'am, we don't want to take much of your time, but we'd be grateful for any help you can give us." The men nodded solemnly to each other as they pored over the map.

Miss Emily gave the map a quick glance. "First thing, you ought to know, you've got this map upside down." She turned the map around for them.

"Of course," Claude squinted down at the map. "The light in here is a little dim for reading."

While Miss Emily's fingers traced a fallen bridge and overgrown dirt roads, Claude scrawled furiously on the map. As soon as the men recorded Miss Emily's information, they left.

She watched them from the window, and then, she turned to us. "Girls, what did you notice about those two men?"

"I have never heard the word "ma'am" spoken by anybody with a northern accent."

Keach laughed. "Wilbur acted as jittery as a turkey the day before Thanksgiving."

"Surveyors?" Miss Emily pounced on the word. "Surveyors work outdoors and stay tanned year-round. I have never seen any surveyors as pale as those two." She turned again to look out the window. "Their faces haven't been kissed by the sun in years. If they turn out to be surveyors, I'll give you back the five dollars you're going to pay me for this album."

"Three dollars." Keach removed the album from the cover and pointed to a small spot near the center. "We found a scratch near the end."

Miss Emily's shoulders slumped in mock despair. "You girls sure make life hard for a poor old lady trying to earn a dime. I'll let you steal this album for four dollars and not a penny less."

"Done!" I shouted.

Outside the shop, Keach bopped me on the head with the album. "Why did you agree so fast? I could have gotten her down to three-fifty, easy."

I shook my head. Keach's love of money bothered me more than surveyors without tans.

Chapter Seven

Sunday Morning Thief

Sunday afternoon, a gentle peace hung over the countryside. Aromas from fried chicken and fresh baked pies poured like incense from farm kitchen windows. While we finished our sausage and biscuits, Grandpa and I thumbed through several *National Geographic* magazines he'd found at a thrift shop a few days earlier. I liked reading the stories about people in other places and imagining how life would be if I were a kid in another country. Also, at the moment, reading about people far away took my mind off the problem of Grandpa's vase. Right there in front of me were stories about Mexico and ancient Greece, along with an article about Indiana hill people, herbs, and bluegrass music.

"Look, Gramps. Here's a picture of a girl about my age fishing in a stream. This issue has pictures of ordinary folks like you and me between pictures of strange people in faraway places."

Grandpa leaned across the table and studied the pictures. "Ordinary? You think we're ordinary? Those people in Greece and Mexico think they are the ordinary ones. To them we are the strange people in a faraway place."

For a minute, I imagined being an ordinary teenager hanging out on the Acropolis in ancient Greece. Thanks to the stories in the magazines, we finished eating without either of us mentioning the vase.

As we washed the last of our dishes, Keach pounded on the back door. "Buddie, we gotta talk." She motioned for me to open the screen door. Outside, away from Grandpa, she jabbered, "Gone! Swiped in broad daylight!"

When I shook my head and waved my hands, she took a deep breath and started over. "I heard the whole story when Pa sent me to buy bread at Popper's Market. Last Friday night, Miss Emily told Mrs. Nelson your vase is worth a pretty penny. Mrs. Nelson couldn't find you or Lutie, so she took the vase home and locked it in her dining room cupboard. This morning, after she went off to church, a thief busted in and stole Lutie's vase. Lots of folks are over at her place right now, waiting for the sheriff to decide what to do next." Keach pulled at my elbow. "Get Lutie and come back over there with me."

I turned away from her. "I can't. Grandpa still doesn't know Miss Emily wants to talk to him. You go on. Come back later and tell me what happens."

"Do you think you can hide out here forever?" She ran off before I answered.

After Keach left, I sat alone on the back porch steps and waited for a long time. Keach didn't return, and I still had to face Grandpa. When I heard him shuffle to the screen door behind me, I did not turn around.

"Everything okay?" he asked.

I nodded, even though nothing was okay. A lump in my throat kept me from telling him a thief had his vase.

"Feel like working?"

"Sure," I nodded again which counted as another fib.

"Bring the calfskin from the water trough in with you."

Before going inside, I pulled the supple skin out of the water trough on the back porch. Grandpa wanted to use this skin to cover the head of a banjo we were making. Soaking in water made the skin softer and easier to cut. I grabbed an old towel draped on the railing and dried the translucent hide. Still, water dripped all over the floor on my way into the front room.

Grandpa knelt and spread the calfskin on the floor while he whistled "Rocky Top" beneath his breath. He placed the maple rim of a banjo we'd started a few weeks earlier in the center and handed me a piece of charcoal. I drew a circle larger than the rim, picked up a pair of shears, and began cutting out the circle.

I took a deep breath. "Guess I should have told you sooner. People have been asking questions about your vase."

He stopped whistling. "What people?"

"Miss Emily."

"Emily? Of course," he repeated softly, leaning back on his heels. "I figured she'd see the vase and be curious."

"You're right. She'll be stopping by to ask you a few questions." Taking an even deeper breath I added, "Mr. Webb mentioned the vase too."

"What did he say?"

I kept my eyes on the shears, trying hard to concentrate. "Not much. He wanted to know if you have anything else you'd like to get rid of. He'll be happy to help you with an auction."

"I bet he would. That man never misses anything worth more than ten cents. Of course, that's because of the business he's in."

"No need for Mr. Webb or anybody else to wonder about your vase now."

"Why?"

"A thief broke into Mrs. Nelson's house this morning. The vase is gone."

Grandpa's hand shook when he tried to fit the neck for the banjo into the rim.

"I'm sorry, Gramps. I'm really, really sorry about giving the vase away without asking. This is all my fault."

He sighed. "Don't fret too much. Our vase might find a way home when the time is right. Let's put this banjo away and make a pot of vegetable soup for supper."

Late that afternoon, as we finished eating our bowls of soup, I dared to ask the one question Grandpa might not want to answer. "Where did we get an old vase worth money?"

Before he answered, Keach came running up on the front porch. She waited, peering through the screen door with her face cupped in her hands, and her nose pressed against the screen.

"Never mind for now. Go on out there before Keach's nose pokes a hole in the screen." Grandpa took my bowl to the sink. "I've got business to take care of in here. We'll talk later."

To keep moths and mosquitoes from buzzing in, I squeaked the door open barely wide enough to squeeze out. Keach and I walked a little way into the front yard.

"What happened this afternoon?" I asked as I sat on the dry brown grass.

"Nothing. Everybody sort of waited for you and Lutie to show up. I told them you weren't too concerned, and we'd be keeping our eyes open."

"Wonderful. That was a stroke of genius. Everybody must have been super-duper excited to hear first-rate detectives like us are on top of the case." I grabbed a handful of withered grass and blew the dry pieces at her.

"I thought you weren't going to go around helping me out anymore."

"Don't blame me. People need to know you're not sitting still with a thief roaming about."

We heard Miss Emily's van clattering down the road long before the headlights came into view. The white van with the words "Emily's Attic" and a mural of her store painted on the side roared into the yard in a cloud of dust and startled crickets. She hopped out wearing her denim shirtwaist dress with tennis shoes to match, and walked up the front path. She waved to Keach and me.

"Evening, Emily." Grandpa stepped onto the porch and offered her one of the two rocking chairs. "I've been expecting you."

"Then you know why I'm here."

Keach and I moved back toward the house and sat on the porch steps. The creaking of the rocking chairs on the far end of the porch covered most of Grandpa and Miss Emily's conversation. Snatches of sentences drifted over us.

"Where on earth?" Miss Emily's voice rose barely above a whisper. "Besides the vase?"

Curious, I strained to hear Grandpa's answer, but couldn't. The rocking chairs creaked in unison. Their conversation grew hushed as if they spoke from the back pew of a church. Sentences grew further apart with words like "crops" and "long dry spell" passing between them.

A bike rattled down the road bearing Adam out of the twilight and across the grass. He stood on the pedals and bounced over a hole before jumping off. After saying hi to everybody, he sat in the space on the steps between Keach and me.

"Buddie, I'm sorry about the vase. I heard Keach say the two of you will be looking for the thief. I'll be glad to help."

Grandpa stopped rocking. "You kids can keep your eyes and ears open, but don't go messing around trying to find the thief by yourselves. Let the sheriff do his job."

Keach shrugged. "I just said that to make people feel better."

Adam leaned toward me. "Sorry I upset Lutie. I only meant to stop and see how you were doing."

People say you can never step in the same river twice. I don't think that's true as far as real friendship goes. Adam's company felt as natural as if he paid us a visit every day.

"Thanks." I picked at a bit of peeling paint on the porch step. "I already upset Grandpa before people got here, but he'll be okay. He hasn't told me anything about the vase. I keep hoping for a chance to ask him a few questions."

Then Mrs. Bonnie Nelson's orange Ford Pinto pulled into the yard. She parked behind Miss Emily and stepped onto the porch. Grandpa stood and motioned for her to take his rocking chair while he leaned against the porch rail.

She sat and rocked slowly back and forth. "Lutie, I'm so sorry. The vase is lovely, but I never gave a thought to the monetary value. Buddie, I'll bet you had no idea of the cash value, either."

The adults all turned to look at us kids. I shook my head.

Grandpa plucked a piece of parsley from a pot on the porch. He chewed thoughtfully for a moment. "Don't go beating yourself up. Thieves take what they want without caring who they hurt. The thief would just have easily stolen the vase from us. Bonnie, the thief knew the best time to break into your house."

It sounded strange to hear Grandpa call Mrs. Nelson by her first name. He slapped at a mosquito near his ear. I wondered if he wanted people to go home and leave us alone. As for me, I tried to think of how to get everyone except Adam to leave.

"There are a few in Whistler who might want to steal your vase," Miss Emily stopped her rocking chair and leaned forward, "but I can't think of anybody willing to risk breaking in and stealing on a Sunday morning."

"Maybe strangers stole the vase." Keach spoke up from her spot on the other side of Adam. "What about the two men in town calling themselves surveyors? What if they're really crooks? Pa told me plenty of people buy antiques dirt cheap in the country. Later, they sell them for huge profits in cities. Think how rich thieves could get stealing antiques and then selling them."

Mrs. Nelson sat still in her chair and folded her hands in her lap. "Lutie, you may be right, but I'm with Keach. I simply can't bear to think anyone in Whistler would do such a thing."

Miss Emily sighed. "I'd rather believe an outsider is the thief."

Mrs. Nelson stood. "My husband went fishing yesterday, and he won't be back until tomorrow. I'm going over to my sister's house in Rockport until Ned gets back. I won't stay home alone with a thief on the loose."

The three of us kids moved off the steps to let her pass. She backed her car out of the yard and drove away.

Grandpa sagged against the porch railing and folded his arms. "Best not to jump to conclusions, but the two strangers ought to be questioned if they haven't already skipped town. Does Sheriff Freeman know about those men?"

Miss Emily rose from her rocker. "I called him right after they left the shop. I suspect there's more to Claude and Wilbur than they let on, but the sheriff can't arrest anyone without proof. They can spread their story about being surveyors all they want, but for my money, 'that dog won't hunt.' Sooner or later, they'll slip up. If we keep our eyes open, we'll find out the real reason they're here."

Grandpa moved toward the door. "We'll all think better after a good night's sleep."

Miss Emily fumbled with her keys. "I really must be going too. Can I give either of you kids a ride home?"

Keach jumped at a chance to ride in the van, but Adam said he wanted to stay a little longer. Keach's eyes widened, and I think mine did too. My heart skipped a couple of beats. I looked away, hoping Adam hadn't noticed the look between Keach and me.

After Keach and Miss Emily left, Grandpa opened the screen door. "Buddie, I've got some work to finish. You can stay out here for a while, but don't be too late." He went inside, leaving me alone with Adam on the porch steps.

Chapter Eight

Alone with a Butterfly

Fireflies danced in the dark. A rustling beneath a nearby bush signaled a night critter foraging for supper.

Adam wasted no time getting to what both of us were thinking.

"So, who do you think took the vase?"

"The only ones I can think of are the two strangers. Miss Emily knew right away they weren't surveyors. They sure acted jumpy in her shop yesterday."

Adam looked off into the distance where a sliver of pink sunset hung above the horizon. "The problem is, if they are professional crooks, adults will be suspicious. Nobody will think much of a kid my age hanging around."

"If they wouldn't think anything about you snooping, they'd pay even less attention to me."

Adam shook his head. "On second thought, maybe I'm wrong. Didn't Lutie say he doesn't want us getting mixed up in this?"

"You're changing your mind because I want to help, but you don't understand." I leaned closer to Adam, and our hands touched. "Don't you see? This is all my fault. I didn't ask Grandpa's permission to give away his vase. I need to find the thief and bring the vase home more than you or anybody else."

"Okay, but we'll have to be careful." Adam paused, looked down at my hand, and changed the subject. "Remember how we used to run around in the woods before you got so busy last summer?"

"Me? I'm not the one who didn't have time to hang out. What about Courtney?"

"Courtney?" Adam's nervous half-smile spread across this face. "After Keach moved in, you were always hanging out with her. I never understood why the two of you turned out to be good friends."

"I don't know. We're different, but maybe I like her because she's always trying to dream big stuff into her life. Also, I think I know how much she misses her mom." I shut my mouth then, embarrassed for telling Adam so much. "You didn't answer my question about Courtney."

"I got lonesome. No girl ever chased me before, and I liked all the attention." He turned to me. "Didn't you ever get a gift that surprised you?"

"No. Never, ever have I been surprised with a gift. I've seen lots of amazing stuff for sale in stores. Though I always knew nothing fancy was meant for me."

"Wanting and getting can turn out to be two different things." Adam paused. "I didn't know hanging out with Courtney meant I couldn't have other friends. Anyway, after our ride home yesterday, she said her mama told her to keep her options open going into high school. Courtney doesn't want to hang out so much anymore, and that's okay by me. Don't you see, Buddie? I miss my friends. I miss ... you."

"Dumped? You got dumped by Courtney!" I laughed.

"Yeah, I guess my first ever girlfriend dumped me, and all I feel is relieved." He reached for my hand and turned the palm up. “We’re a lot alike.” He rubbed the tips of my fingers. “The skin on your fingertips is rough from picking a mandolin. My fingertips are the same way from playing my guitar.”

“Oh? My fingertips are rough? Is that your idea of a compliment?” I teased him, hoping he wouldn’t hear my heart thumping because we were, basically, holding hands. He laughed, and we sat there together enjoying the moment without saying another word.

“Our music is sure different,” I said. “That kind of music sounds rich and far away like the pictures I’ve seen in Grandpa’s *National Geographic* magazines. Your music makes me think about all the places I want to go someday. The way you play is strong and sure, not shy like—”

“Like you?”

The warmth of a blush crept up my neck and over my face.

Pointing to a clump of black-eyed Susans growing beside the steps, he added, “Or shy like that butterfly?”

With wings closed, half hidden among the leaves, an orange and black monarch butterfly clung to a stem. In the long summer twilight, the butterfly appeared to be made of velvet.

“Not like that butterfly. Monarchs are strong enough to fly from here to Mexico.”

“With those wings?”

“I read about them in one of our *National Geographics*. They migrate like birds to Mexico. I saw pictures of millions of them covering trees in one special place.”

Letting go of my hand, Adam plucked the flower stem with the butterfly resting serene and majestic. He held the stem within inches of my face. The butterfly’s wings opened slowly once, twice. Lifting into the evening, the fragile wings fluttered west. We watched the monarch fade into the night, and then, Grandpa began coughing and stomping around inside the house.

"Do you think he's hinting for me to leave?" Adam whispered.

I smiled. "Maybe we can pretend we didn't hear him."

"That's okay," Adam walked toward his bike. "I'd rather stay on his good side. Remember the farm we talked about? Will you meet me there tomorrow after lunch?"

I nodded. "I'll be there."

Adam pedaled away with his bike headlight marking a bumpy path over the grass and down the road. Grandpa came to the screen door. "Can you come in and give me a hand?"

I rose slowly, savoring Adam's visit before going inside. I thought Grandpa wanted help with the banjo we had been making earlier. Instead, we went into his bedroom where he had thrown a pile of junk on his lumpy bed. I recognized an ivory-handled letter opener we saved to use on our winning sweepstakes notice. Next to the letter opener was a small metal box he kept under his bed. One summer long ago, I saw him open the box and lift out a piece of smudged paper. He quickly replaced the paper and closed the box when he saw me watching him.

Near his pillow, Grandpa placed a flax hackle and a little loom he had let me use one summer to weave tiny rugs. I always thought the loom and hackle must have belonged to my grandmother. At the foot of the bed, I saw a crumbling leather-bound book with the title *Aesop's Fables* lettered in gold on the cover. A brown and green snuff bottle and an old rifle we called Mariah rounded out the pile on the bed. To me, these were no more than everyday items around the house.

"What's all this stuff doing in here?" I asked, moving to the bed and picking up the book.

"None of this is junk." Grandpa rubbed his hands carefully over the polished rifle stock. "I know you're curious, but tonight I'm all talked out." He handed me a stack of newspapers and set his jaw in a way I knew meant asking questions would make things worse. After we carefully wrapped each piece and bundled everything except the metal box into two burlap sacks, he said, "Come early morning, we'll be taking to the woods. Off to bed with you now."

I welcomed crawling between my sheets, but wondering what Grandpa might be up to made sleep hard to find.

Chapter Nine

Abe Lincoln's Secret

Before daybreak, Grandpa's alarm clock jangled on the floorboards beside his bed. I dozed off again until the smell of coffee and simmering oatmeal pulled me from beneath the covers. Grandpa had finished eating before I sat at the table.

Questions swarmed inside my brain like hornets stirred with a stick. I knew better than to ask for answers. Grandpa never liked to be rushed, especially about anything important. If I stayed quiet and let him gather his thoughts, eventually he'd tell me everything. Meanwhile, I tried to eat, though pieces of my life had been jerked out of place.

Grandpa's gnarled fingers curled and uncurled around his white coffee mug. Age spots covered the back of his hands. The dry skin on his knuckles shone the same way the mandolins and banjos he kept for us had turned shiny with use. He seldom tried to play anymore because the old tools he used for shaping wood split his nails and bruised his hands. Trying to play with his battered hands left him frustrated. Music still ran through his mind and often erupted in whistling or humming while he worked.

The stubble on his chin always quivered before he shared anything important, and now his chin trembled over his coffee. Elbows resting on the table, he leaned forward. "Long time ago, before your ma brought you here, I went looking for 'sang near Dry Branch Gulley."

That was nothing new. Each autumn we searched for ginseng, the wild herb we called 'sang, with roots sometimes growing in the shape of a twisted old man. Careful eyes spotted red berries hoisted like a signal topping the ginseng plant. Grandpa knew where to find this valuable herb in rich pockets of earth deep in the woods. We dug out the roots, sold them, and tried to make the money last till Christmas. In addition to selling instruments at the festival in Bean Blossom, we usually sold a couple of mandolins or banjos before Christmas to get through the worst of winter.

Grandpa added another spoonful of sugar to his coffee. "Well, one day an old spotted hound I used to have trotted beside me into the woods. After a while, he ran in circles like he caught scent of a rabbit or squirrel. Next thing I knew, the dog disappeared like the earth opened and swallowed him whole.

"He had to be close, but I couldn't find one hair of him. When he started yelping, I figured he'd gotten stuck inside a bush. After poking around here and there, a big clump of bushes at the base of a hill gave way. Brush completely covered a three-foot-high cave hole in the base of a hill above the gulley rim. You see, the dog fell in and couldn't climb out. I pulled him free, came home for a light, and went back by myself."

"How come you never showed me this cave?"

"I've got my reasons. That small limestone cave turned out to be shaped like a piece of pie. Sloping up, down, and sideways back from the entrance, the hole made a deep, dry pocket in the earth. Straight back about thirty feet, the space opened to ten feet high and maybe twenty feet wide.

The cave turned out to be a small pocket in the side of the hill."

"So what? There's lots of those pocket caves in these woods."

Grandpa gave me a stern look. "Hush. I'm trying to tell you what I should have told you a long time ago."

Nodding, I made a zipping motion across my mouth with my fingers and waited.

"Against the back wall of that cave, I found a trunk like the ones pioneers hauled on wagons. All the stuff we packed last night, and the vase you gave Bonnie Nelson, came out of that trunk. For years, we've had these things hidden in plain sight in this house under everybody's nose. I kept all of it exactly the way the Lincoln family wanted. Before anything else goes missing, we'll hide what we still have back in the trunk in the cave."

"Lincoln? What Lincoln family?" By now, Grandpa had me sitting on the edge of my chair. "Who are you talking about, and how are they connected to the trunk in the cave?"

Grandpa went into his room and came back with the little metal box. He opened the lid and unfolded the fragile paper. With his hand shaking, he gave me what appeared to be a handwritten note. Not more than six inches wide and eight inches long, the note bore several stains, and bugs had chewed the corners. The faded ink and odd, old-fashioned spelling made the note hard to read, but I managed to make sense of most of the words.

> March 1, 1830
> Family of T. Lincoln moving on to Illinois. Road half frozen, Ox stuk in mud. To ease wagon load we leef trunk in this here cave. Will fetch next year. Shud we not return, finder welcome to keep goodes. Ask only finder

> value our treasures and keep these safe. We are poor people seeking better life. One person's life is forever worth more than any goodes. A. Lincoln.

"A. Lincoln? Wait ... Abraham Lincoln? *That* Lincoln?" At Grandpa's nod, I said, "Sure 'nuff, those old things must be worth a fortune." I looked from Grandpa back to the note. My brain struggled to grasp the fact that Grandpa's hands and mine were the first to touch Abe's handwriting in nearly one hundred and fifty years. Lincoln's own fingerprints might still be pressed all over the paper. I dropped the note on the table and stared at the writing.

Grandpa retrieved the fragile paper and replaced it in the metal box as he continued his story. "Abraham's father, Thomas Lincoln, married Sarah Bush after Abe's mother died. Sarah couldn't read or write, but rumor said she liked nice things. Sarah's first husband had also died, so she brought household goods from her first marriage. My guess is at least part of the contents of the trunk belonged to her."

My heart plummeted. "I can't believe I gave away Abraham Lincoln's vase. Sorry, Gramps, so, so sorry!" I buried my face in my hands.

Grandpa patted my arm. "Be quiet and let me finish. When Abe was twenty-one, he helped his family move from their home near here to Illinois. In early March, roads would have been muddy and half-frozen. The Lincolns were probably desperate to make the wagon easier for the ox to pull. Abe knew these woods well. I'm thinking he discovered that cave earlier. If my dog hadn't fallen in, his trunk might never have been found."

With dollar signs in my eyes, I rubbed my hands together. "The law says finders, keepers, right?"

"First, I paid a visit to a lawyer to ask about ownership. I didn't show him anything from the trunk. I handwrote a copy of the note without including the owner and explained I'd found items on my property I thought to be of historical value. According to the lawyer, the letter clearly states if the owners didn't return, the trunk and the contents belong to the finder. We are the guardians of the Lincoln's lost belongings. All these years, I've honored Lincoln's wishes by keeping the note and his family treasures safe."

"How much is all this stuff worth?"

Grandpa swallowed the last of his coffee and rinsed his mug in the sink. "You've seen the problems the vase caused even without people knowing the original owner. If you're talking about money, I don't know. Maybe the note is worth more than everything else put together."

The spoonful of oatmeal I held in my hand fell back into the bowl. "We could buy everything we need with that kind of cash. How valuable are we talking here?"

Grandpa shrugged. "Depends on what you mean by value. Some of the items may be worth plenty of money. If the letter does turn out to be Abraham Lincoln's, the cash value is more than folks like us can imagine." He leaned heavily on the back of his chair. "Anyway, that kind of talk is about money. We're not going to bother ourselves where cash is concerned. People worry me more. Saul and Emily both recognized the vase had value without knowing it belonged to the Lincolns. The thief saw the possibility of money as well. Now everybody knows. Money-hungry people will come snooping, trying to see what else we have in here."

So, with the vase gone, Grandpa believed he had failed to keep the treasures safe the way Lincoln wanted. "Why didn't you tell me all of this sooner?"

"Thought I'd tell you the whole story when you decided what to do after high school. You've talked about going to college. If you want more education, Lincoln's belongings might be the ticket to your future. After you gave Mrs. Nelson the vase, telling you got a whole lot harder. I knew how bad you'd feel when you realized what you did."

"You're right. I felt plain awful before. Now I feel double rotten." Suddenly my oatmeal didn't seem so appealing. I pushed the bowl away.

"Don't waste time stewing over what we can't change. The main problem now is to protect the note and all we have left. For over a hundred years, nothing more than cobwebs touched Lincoln's trunk. We'll put everything, except the metal box and note, back in the cave until we figure out what to do next."

He motioned for me to follow him into my bedroom where he reached under my bed and pulled out two stacks of *National Geographic* magazines to make an empty space. Stretching out on the floor, he pushed the box with Lincoln's note into the space and replaced the stacks of magazines around the box.

"Thieves will search my room first. Nobody will guess you have anything of value."

How could he be so sure? Wouldn't a thief look everywhere? And, how could I possibly sleep at night with Abraham Lincoln's note right there under my bed?

Chapter Ten

Voices in the Woods

After we cleared the table, each of us picked up one of the burlap bags and headed into the woods. The sun rose and hung above the horizon like a golden egg yolk. Most of the time, I liked walking with Grandpa through the deep woods in the early morning. We often trod softly looking for small game in one of the traps he set. Other times, we scrounged for plants we might be able to use or sell. Grandpa always said God gives us the right gift in the moment of our greatest need. We only must be sharp enough to recognize and use those gifts. Sure enough, like the ginseng, we usually found what we needed in our own woods.

We had not gone far when Grandpa took a bulb of garlic from his pocket, peeled a clove, and stuck the raw garlic in his mouth.

"Your chest bothering you again?"

"Off and on. Long as I keep a bit of garlic handy, the pain eases up."

Even though I shifted my sack from one arm to the other, a heavy ache settled between my shoulder blades. "Where is this place?"

"We'll be there soon. Did I ever tell you about the time I played music at Bean Blossom with Bill Monroe himself?"

"Not lately."

Grandpa chewed his garlic. "Nearly everybody who came to the festival played an instrument. Banjos, guitars, fiddles, mandolins, and dulcimers were everywhere. Some had a harmonica stuffed in the hip pocket of their jeans." He paused, leaned against a tree and wheezed for a few seconds.

"You okay, Grandpa?"

"Yep. Let me catch my breath."

After three or four minutes, we walked on, a little slower than before, while he continued his story.

"One old woman made the craziest music with nothing but a washboard. I wandered about, looking for players joining up in twos or threes, picking snatches of tunes whenever the fancy hit me.

"Late one afternoon, I found a shady spot beneath an oak to pick bits of tunes by myself. Soon, a man with a fiddle and a gal with a dulcimer stopped by and asked to play along. We took up '"Fox on the Run"' while a knot of folks gathered round for hand clappin' and foot stompin'. Right then, Bill Monroe stepped up. When he asked to join us, we brought him in without skippin' a lick. An hour or so later, he says to me, 'You're a mighty fine mandolin player.'"

The smile on Grandpa's face told me he enjoyed remembering the casual compliment given to him by the father of bluegrass music. "Are we going to Bean Blossom this year?" I asked.

He turned to me with a gleam in his eyes. "I've already found us a ride. Emily is going to an auction up that way the Saturday of the festival week. If you forget about the vase and work hard on your music between now and then, we'll hitch a ride with her."

I began thinking about songs I wanted to practice, and before long we stood above the empty creek bed called Dry Branch Gulley. The deep trench divided the back acres of our land from Saul Webb's. Grandpa once told me the gulley had been dry ever since a fierce storm called a "gulley washer" back in 1910. He was just a boy then.

An out-of-place mound rose a few inches above the dry creek bed in the gulley. The mound marked an abandoned underground room concealed by a trapdoor made of wood, dirt, and grass. Only the sharp eyes of a woodsman might notice the unusual rise in the bottom of the gulley.

Forty years earlier, bootleggers made moonshine whiskey in the dugout room under the creek bed. Federal agents had removed the equipment long ago, but beneath the trap door the underground room remained. Grandpa revealed the hidden room to Adam and me a few summers earlier, cautioning us never to climb in there by ourselves. We honored his request, but now and then we pulled the trap door aside and peered in. The summer before, I also tugged the door open to show Keach how moonshiners hid their still.

Now, looking back up at the brush growing along the edge of the hill above the gulley, I tried to guess where Lincoln's cave might be hidden.

"Bet you'll never find the entrance," Grandpa teased.

"Give me a minute." I studied the hillside, then pointed. "You mentioned the cave is hidden at the base of a little hill." I walked to where the brush grew thickest. Spider webs strung among the weeds glistened like tiny bridges made of diamonds. I jumped when a toad hopped out from the dew-moistened grass. Tough stems of dainty Queen

Anne's lace gave off a heavy green-herb scent when I twisted them away from the hill. Almost ready to give up, I heard loose pebbles tumbling downward. When I pulled aside a thick tangle of brush, the entrance stared back at me like a large dark eye at the base of the hill.

"Good for you," Grandpa said, sliding inside feet first. I followed and pulled the sacks in behind us. At first, roots poked through chinks in the rocks and clawed like skinny, dead fingers, scratching at my arms, grabbing at my hair. The inside of the cave quickly opened up until our flashlight played on a long, low wooden trunk against the limestone wall at the far end. Warmth from the earth made the air smell alive. The trunk's crumbled leather hinges gave no sound when we lifted the lid.

After we packed Lincoln's treasures inside and covered them with the empty burlap bags, Grandpa reached back in the trunk and pulled out the old rifle. "Mariah might come in handy. She'll stay with us."

"What good is a busted rifle?"

"We're the only ones who know this rifle is broken."

Grandpa closed the trunk and walked back toward the patch of light marking the entrance. Less than four feet from the mouth of the cave, he stopped short. I smacked my nose against his bony spine. "Grandpa!"

He turned sharply and clamped his hand over my mouth.

Muffled voices filtered into the cave from the hilltop above our heads.

"At least fifty dollars more. Give me that much or the deal's off."

A second voice cursed. "It ain't worth that much."

The hair on the back of my neck stood up as footsteps shuffled through the leaves. We waited, scarcely breathing, until we heard nothing more than the sound of our own breath. When we crawled out, both the men and their footsteps had vanished in the morning mist rising from the woodland floor.

Grandpa bent down with his face close to my ear. "Listen to me. Tell nobody about what we've hidden out here."

I figured he meant especially not to tell Keach, and I didn't like secrets. "Can't we get Mr. Webb to sell all of Lincoln's goods, and we'll keep the money? Instead of worrying about fixing the lock on the back door, we'll build a whole new house."

"You still don't see. Saul wouldn't care about who gets the Lincoln family goods. He'd auction pieces off separately because with him money is the main goal. Each piece the Lincolns left behind had value for them. Everything in the trunk means more than money to me. We have to find people who will take care of what the Lincolns left behind. For now, everything except the vase is safe while we decide what to do." He pointed his finger at my nose. "One more thing: don't ever let me hear of you getting the true value of anything mixed up with money."

Grandpa wheezed most of the way back home. We stopped often for him to lean against a tree, catch his breath, and eat more garlic. Safe inside our house, he wiped his forehead and slumped in his wicker chair by the woodstove in the front room. I lifted my mandolin from a peg by the door and played a few whispers of "Amazing Grace." He dozed for a few minutes and then snorted and rubbed his face.

I decided to ask the question that had bothered me all the way home. "What did you think about those men we heard talking out there in the woods?"

"My guess is they were hunters. Lots of folks go through the woods early in the morning."

"They were arguing. What if they were fighting over our vase?"

Grandpa shook his head and laughed. "Two men at odds while they're out hunting don't make them thieves. After all, what if they'd caught us sneaking out of the cave? What would they be thinking about us?"

Chapter Eleven

A Break in the Case

We ate bologna sandwiches for lunch. While I washed our plates, Grandpa went back to his chair where he promptly fell asleep. After hiding the rifle on my closet shelf, I changed into white shorts and a black T-shirt. With hurried strokes, I brushed my hair a hundred times and ran the comb through long and straight.

Keach had given me a free sample of Watermelon Frost lipstick she got from an Avon lady. I rummaged in my shirt drawer and dug out the lipstick. After covering my mouth with Watermelon Frost, I licked my lips. The bright color made my face seem pale. For good measure, I smeared a tiny dab of Watermelon Frost on each cheek. I used my fingertips to spread the color over my cheeks, rubbing until the bit of color looked like a natural blush.

White shorts were a mistake for doing farm work. I ripped off the shorts, flung them on the bed, and pulled on a pair of jeans. I changed my mind about my hair too and plaited one long braid before running out the door. With any luck, I'd be at the farm before mid-afternoon.

An "Abraham Lincoln Boyhood Home" sign pointed the way along a path to a clearing in the woods. The pounding of hammers and rasping of saws grew louder as I ran between the trees leading to the farm. A crude log cabin surrounded by a half-finished rail fence stood in a clearing. Not a single blade of grass grew in the packed red earth between the fence and cabin. I watched from behind a tree and looked for Adam.

Three girls chased chickens escaping from a pen behind the cabin. Two boys stacked firewood near the chicken yard, while a girl stretched a deerskin over the outside cabin wall.

As I tried to get up the nerve to leave the safety of the tree, Adam walked out of the cabin toward a wooden barrel filled with water beneath one corner of the roof. He dipped a hollow gourd into the barrel and poured water into a bucket. Courtney came strolling out of the chicken pen, grabbed the gourd, and dumped water over Adam's head. He dropped the bucket making water spill in a dark streak across the earth. Courtney's hair whipped around her face and they both laughed when Adam made a grab for the gourd.

I imagined myself punching Courtney in the nose. What would Adam think if I did? The only other option would be to make a run for home. Turning, I fled and kept going, trying not to cry. I dashed behind the buildings in town, hoping no one saw me.

A sharp pain in my side forced me to stop and catch my breath beneath a tree. I sat, leaned against the tree trunk, and rolled up my jeans. Sweat plastered stubby blonde hair against my knees. For the last year, I'd secretly shaved my legs whenever Grandpa put a new blade in his razor. Courtney, of course, probably had her own razor. Bet she started shaving her legs in kindergarten. Maybe I'd get Grandpa's razor again the next time he went outside to cut wood. With my side still hurting, I headed toward Miss Emily's store thinking I'd grab a few minutes of cool air before going the rest of the way home.

As I opened the door, the sleigh bells jangled. Behind the counter, Miss Emily made short jumps as she tried to reach three boxes on a shelf.

"Hi, Miss Emily. Can I give you a hand?"

She turned to face me. "Hi, Buddie. Your timing is perfect. If you can bring down those boxes, I won't have to find a step stool."

Most of the eighth graders were taller than Miss Emily. She often asked us to get things on higher shelves. Standing on tiptoes, I stretched my arms and lowered the boxes she wanted.

"Why don't you stay and help me unpack?" She opened the flaps on the first box. "I love finding treasures." Out came four old picture albums full of black and white and sepia-toned photos. She slowly turned the brittle pages. "All these people were loved by someone. The person who made this album wanted their family to be remembered. Too bad they didn't put names with the pictures."

I ran my fingers across a photo of a woman in a wide hat with a drooping feather. "What do you think happened to all these people? The photos are so old, none of them are alive now."

Miss Emily stopped turning the pages. In an off-hand tone of voice, she said, "Oh, they're all still alive."

Goose bumps prickled on my arms. Was it the air conditioning or wondering what she meant about those people being alive? "That's impossible! Look, here's a man in a Civil War uniform."

"Nothing's impossible."

"They're all alive?"

"Yep. Luke 20:38 tells us, God isn't God of the dead. He is God of the living because to God, everybody is alive."

"Well, then, where are they?"

"Oh, Buddie." She sighed. "We make things so complicated, but of this, I am sure—there is another world beyond this one. Don't you know? The love of Christ is the wind we ride from this world into the nex—"

The doorbell jangled. In barged Claude and Wilbur.

Miss Emily stiffened beside me.

"Afternoon, Miss Emily," Claude mopped his brow with his handkerchief. "You were so helpful the other day, we're hoping you have time to give us a little more information."

"That depends," Miss Emily replied with an icy tone. She dropped the photo album we'd been admiring onto a chair. "What kind of information do you need?"

Claude unfolded their map on the counter. "Can you tell us how to get out to a place called the Everett farm? A friend of ours is looking to buy a few acres. We understand the farmhouse has been vacant for some time. Could you show us the best roads to take?"

Miss Emily smoothed the map. "Sure thing. Always glad to help a couple of, um ... surveyors. Roads out that way can be overgrown. Here, let me show you the route you ought to take." She traced the longest route possible out to the abandoned farm.

I tapped Miss Emily's arm and whispered, "I need to get home."

She gave me a wink and a nod, and I took off running. Five minutes later, I slammed our front door and startled Grandpa awake in his chair.

"What's gotten into you?"

"Bet those so-called surveyors took our vase. They're going out to snoop around the old Everett place." I closed my bedroom door and grabbed Mariah from my closet shelf. With a little push, my window screen fell onto the grass. I set the rifle down in a patch of dandelions and backed out of the window. When I turned to pick up the rifle, I found nothing.

The next thing I knew, Grandpa'd grabbed me by the neck of my T-shirt. He held the rifle out of my reach. "Where do you think you're going with this?"

"I can't hurt those crooks with a broken rifle, but I can scare them. How else can I stop them?"

"If they are thieves, they won't be afraid of you, no matter what you carry. If they're honest, you'll get yourself in a mess of trouble trying to scare them."

I struggled against Grandpa's grasp, but he held tight. "You mean I can't go? You're going to let them get away with stealing more than our vase?"

"No. Of course not. We'll hike out there together."

Grandpa let go of my shirt, and we took off walking. Revived by the nap in his chair, he still couldn't move as fast as I wanted. Soon, I slowed my steps to match his.

The abandoned Everett farm joined the left back side of our acreage. On the way, I told Grandpa what I'd heard in Miss Emily's shop. He took a clove of garlic from his pocket and began chewing. The sharp smell pierced the air, and I held my breath for a moment.

Grandpa stopped and looked me up and down. "See here, you've told me why you think you need to get over there, but you're still biting your tongue. Look at you, walking straight and stiff, stompin' along like a city gal. What's on your mind?"

"Adam asked me to meet him at the Lincoln farm after lunch today." I kept my face forward, jaw set.

"Did you go?"

"I went."

"Was he there?"

"He was there, flirting with Courtney." Anger rose again in my chest, but with effort I kept my voice casual, as if I didn't care.

"What did you say to him?"

"Nothing."

"What did he say to you?"

I glanced at Grandpa. "Nothing. I left before he saw me."

"What you are saying is nothing happened."

"That's the problem. Remember Abe Lincoln's note? Maybe I'm the one who's stuck, and I need to lighten my load by letting go of Adam."

"Be careful. Adam has a good heart. Both of you are older now, and your friendship might take a different twist. That's natural. Nothing alive ever stays the same."

"All I want right now is to make sure those fake surveyors get what's coming to them."

Chapter Twelve

Nothing to Sneeze At

Several times along the way, Grandpa started wheezing, and we had to stop. At the Everett farm, we walked out of the trees behind the ramshackle barn. I breathed a sigh of relief when I realized Wilbur and Claude's VW was nowhere in sight. The woods ended at the edge of a field where a garden once grew. On the far side of the garden patch, the house stood with part of the roof missing.

Grandpa surveyed the windblown shingles and stray shutters on the ground. "This place is a wreck. Why do you think Claude and Wilbur want to drive out here looking for valuable antiques?"

"Look, Grandpa, they won't know what kind of shape the farm is in until they get here."

His forehead wrinkled until his eyebrows met at the top of his nose. "Don't you see? You never heard them say a word about antiques. You're calling them thieves with nothing to back up what you've already decided."

"What else could they be?"

Grandpa rubbed the stubble on his face. "I'm not sure. Saying they're thieves picks a sour note in me." He popped another piece of garlic into his mouth and walked toward the back of the house.

Ignoring the stench of his breath, I moved in close beside him. "What're we going to do? There's no sense being out here if they're honest."

"We won't know for sure whether you're right or wrong until they get here. Meanwhile, we'll wait inside, out of the heat, until they show up."

At the top of the termite-infested back steps, the unlocked door creaked open on rusty hinges. We brushed away cobwebs and stepped over bits of stove pipe scattered on the kitchen floor. With a heavy sigh, Grandpa sat down on a grimy, sheet-covered sofa in the living room.

I slumped on the floor against the wall beneath the front window. Matchbooks littered the linoleum around the gaping door of an ancient pot-bellied stove. The faint scent of ashes still lingered in the room. In one corner, two sprung mousetraps remained forever empty beside a large mouse hole. Dust covered several worn patches in the linoleum. I imagined the Everett children dancing and playing around a fire crackling in the stove on snowy winter evenings.

Grandpa pointed the rifle down and leaned forward, resting his hands and chin on the gunstock. "You know, I met your grandma right here in this very room." His red-rimmed eyes grew bright with memories. "I first laid eyes on Mary when I brought extra sorghum over to Mrs. Everett. Times were hard back in those days, but people shared. Yessir, Mary came to visit the oldest Everett girl. Though she was younger than me, your grandma was tall and sharp-witted like you.

"She promised to bring my bucket back on her way home. Sure enough, she brought the bucket filled with biscuits she had baked herself. With one bite of those biscuits, she forever stole my heart. I would have followed her anywhere."

Grandpa young and in love? I've never thought about him being young or falling in love with Grandma. The sound of a car rattling toward the house shook my thoughts away from wondering about Grandpa's younger days. I peeked over the window ledge and saw the gold VW stop beside the farm gate. Claude stepped out of the car and quickly walked up the overgrown path while Wilbur puffed along behind him. I scrunched beneath the window. "What happens if they come in here?"

"We'll wait in the kitchen pantry until they leave or until we step out and surprise them."

Grandpa slumped on the sofa and sat with his gun across his knees, ready to move at a moment's notice. I risked another peek over the windowsill. Both men stood with their backs to the porch.

"Where do we start?" Wilbur asked, sounding as if he didn't want to start at all.

"Check outside first," Claude answered. "Search any hiding place like the inside of a cistern or tree stumps. I'll go through the barn."

"You always take the cool indoor places."

"Do what I ask. You'll have less trouble poking around outside than going through these broken-down buildings."

Wilbur shoved his hands into his pockets and kicked at a clump of grass. "Because I'm new at this, you think you can tell me what to do."

"Because you're new at this, I'm letting you search the easy places. Keep your eyes open and try to be useful."

As I watched, Claude walked off toward the barn. As soon as Claude disappeared inside the barn, Wilbur fumbled in his pocket and pulled out a Hershey bar. He backed up and sat on the top porch step. With loud slurping noises, he polished off the sticky chocolate, licked his fingers, then strolled across the yard to investigate a tangle of blackberry bushes. I could have told him the berries wouldn't be ripe for another three weeks. After Wilbur poked around in the green berries, he stretched out in the clover on the shady side of the brambles and pulled his hat down over his face.

A minute or two later, Claude yelled from the barn, "Find anything out there?"

Wilbur rolled over and crawled about as if he might be searching the grass. "No, not yet."

"If the front door is unlocked, go inside the house," Claude shouted. "I'll be right there."

Grandpa motioned for me to follow him. We made our way through the kitchen and settled on a bench in the pantry. The living room door creaked open. We heard Wilbur shuffle in and plop down on the sofa.

Claude soon followed. "Get up. This is no time to sit around."

"You didn't find anything out in that nice cool barn, did you?"

"A few empty cartons, but valuables turn up in the strangest places. What we need to uncover is a major storage point or a pick-up station."

In the dim light filtering through cracks around the pantry door, I looked at Grandpa. He grinned at me, stretched his arms, and fumbled in his overall pocket for a fresh piece of garlic.

"Look, Wilbur, you're missing clues right under your feet. See these footprints in the dust? People made these prints and not long ago."

I remembered the dust on the living room linoleum and realized we left a clear trail straight to the pantry.

"What ... what if they're still here?" Wilbur asked.

"Shhh!" Claude replied.

Footsteps drew closer and stopped on the other side of the kitchen door. At that moment, dust in the pantry and Grandpa's garlic breath sent a powerful tickle through my nose. I struggled to hold my breath. The sneeze exploded, producing a swift silence in the living room. Grandpa patted my shoulder as if to say the sneeze didn't matter. We slipped out of the pantry, and Grandpa pointed the rifle toward the kitchen door.

"Come in here with your hands up," he roared, "or I'll blast both this door and you into the next county."

A scuffling commenced in the other room. Grandpa kicked the door hard, smacking Claude's face. Claude stumbled backward over Wilbur, and both men landed in a tangle on the floor.

"Pr-Private Investigators." Wilbur struggled to pull out his wallet. He managed to reveal his official-looking identity card. From his seat on the floor, Wilbur squinted up at Grandpa. "Now that we caught you, I think you better con-confess your ill-ill-illegal activities."

"Lutie McBride, at your service," Grandpa offered Wilbur a hand to help him up. "I think you've already met my granddaughter, Buddie."

Claude stood without help and brushed dust off his clothes. He regained his dignity and reached forward to take Grandpa's rifle. "Hand over that firearm!"

Grandpa opened his mouth wide and coughed hard directly in Claude's face.

A blast of pure garlic breath sent Claude reeling backward.

Grandpa looked down as if he had forgotten about the rifle. His ribs heaved, and he shook with silent laughter until tears spilled down his face. "Scared you boys, didn't I?" he said as soon as he gained enough control to speak.

"You think this is loaded? This rifle is more than a hundred years old, and she's busted."

"What are you doing out here?" Claude asked.

"We could ask you the same question. Buddie thinks you stole a vase of ours, but I doubt that's the case. You weren't in town long enough to know about the vase or Mrs. Nelson's locked cupboard. I brought Buddie out here to see what happens when you call somebody guilty without asking any questions. Now, I have a question for you. Are you really private investigators?"

Wilbur and Claude exchanged glances. Claude answered, "Maybe you will help us if you understand the real reason we're here."

Grandpa's face turned pale, and his shoulders sagged. A look of concern crossed Claude's face. "Lutie, sit down and rest a minute. We'll check out the other rooms, and then, we'll give you and Buddie a ride home. We'll talk another time."

Grandpa and I sat in the living room until Claude and Wilbur felt satisfied the house held nothing of value. When the two men came back, we followed them to the car.

Claude opened the passenger door. "Wilbur, you and Buddie climb in the backseat. Mr. McBride, you'll be more comfortable up front with me."

After we settled in the car and drove out onto the road, Grandpa told Claude which roads to take for the shortest drive to our house. We rode in silence until Grandpa asked, "Why were the two of you poking around out there?"

Claude hesitated. "I've been a private investigator for fifteen years. This is his first trip." He nodded toward Wilbur. "His uncle owns our agency. I'm supposed to be training him." Then, as if he wanted to change the subject, Claude asked, "Have you seen anybody behaving strangely lately?"

I wondered if Grandpa might tell them about the voices in the woods early that morning.

"Have I seen any strange behavior?" Grandpa turned toward Claude. "I'd say the four of us acted stranger today than anybody I know. If strange behavior is a crime, all of us should be locked up right now."

By then we had reached our house, and Claude laughed. "You're right. Guess we've still got some explaining to do. Can we drop by tomorrow morning and tell you the whole story?"

Chapter Thirteen

Misery

The next morning, we worked outside while we waited for Claude and Wilbur. Grandpa decided we ought to let the men explain themselves outdoors in case they weren't honest after all. As we cut back the zinnias, Grandpa held up a huge, perfect pink flower. "So beautiful," he said. "I see God's fingerprints all over this blossom. Zinnias are sort of like people. They have to be cut back now and then to keep them blooming." We were still cutting zinnias when Claude and Wilbur drove up.

Claude walked halfway across the yard while Wilbur took his time tumbling out of the car. Wilbur still wore the same clothes he had on at the Everett farm the day before, and he looked miserable. With his arms crossed, he scratched furiously at his armpits. Next, he rubbed his waist. Within a few seconds, Wilbur lost all modesty. He clawed at his neck, then his thighs and legs with such vigor I feared he'd shred the clothes off his body.

Claude hurried to where we were cutting flowers. "We've got a problem." He pointed back at Wilbur. "He's been like this since late last night, but says he isn't allergic to anything. Could he have picked up something yesterday at the farm?"

Grandpa sighed. "Poor Wilbur. My guess would be chiggers."

"What'd you say?" Claude asked and Wilbur stopped scratching long enough to give Grandpa his full attention.

"Chiggers. Looks like Wilbur picked up a bad case of chiggers. They're tiny mites that bite the fire out of you."

"Yeah," I tried to sound serious. "Wilbur, you probably got 'em while you were resting in the clover by those blackberry bushes."

"Resting in the clover?" Claude turned to his companion. "Serves you right. I never could catch you loafing on the job. Guess this time you got what you deserve."

Claude, obviously, had never been bitten by chiggers. There are some things nobody deserves.

"You might as well come inside," Grandpa waved his flower cutting scissors toward the back door. "Maybe we can help."

Inside the house, I grabbed a box of Epsom salt, a box of baking soda, and a bottle of calamine lotion from a cabinet in the bathroom along with a clean towel and washcloth. Grandpa brought fresh overalls, underwear, and a T-shirt from his bedroom while I ran warm water in the bathtub.

Grandpa poured ample amounts of baking soda and Epsom salt in the bath water. "Wilbur, before you get in the tub, open the window screen and throw your clothes outside."

A puzzled look crossed Wilbur's face. "All of them?"

"Every stitch. I'll burn them later. These fresh clothes will keep you decent until you get back to the motel. Soak in the tub for a good long while. Then, soap all over and scrub yourself. After you dry off, dab this calamine lotion wherever you itch." Wilbur nodded, desperate enough to try anything.

While we sat in the front room waiting for Wilbur, Claude paced back and forth. He looked first at an almost finished mandolin and banjo leaning against the wall. Next, he picked up a few *Reader's Digest* magazines stacked in the corner and thumbed through a couple of issues. Grandpa didn't say a word and neither did I.

Finally, Claude broke the silence. "You might as well know. We work for a man who collects antique gold and silver jewelry. About a year ago, he put several pieces up for auction. One of his antiques, a diamond-encrusted gold bracelet, went missing before being sold. Six months later, reproductions of his bracelet flooded the market. In the past two years, similar cases have been reported. A small, valuable antique is taken. Later, dozens of reproductions of the stolen antique appear, usually in another part of the country."

"I see," Grandpa put a fresh piece of garlic in his mouth. "The thief makes a double profit. He gets the real thing for free and unloads fakes on unsuspecting buyers. With all the fakes around, tracking the real piece is nearly impossible."

Claude slapped his knee. "Exactly! Because of the locations of the thefts, we think the main operation is in this area."

I leaned forward. "Does Sheriff Freeman know who you really are? Plenty of people might make the same mistake I made."

Claude paused. "After we heard the vase had been stolen, I talked to the sheriff. Your vase fits the pattern of being valuable and small enough to be easily reproduced. The thief might be the same person we're after."

Wilbur eased into the front room. Splotches of pink lotion covered his face and neck. His arms hung like stuffed sausages from the sleeves of Grandpa's T-shirt. The overalls, with Wilbur crammed inside, bulged and strained at every seam.

Claude's face wrinkled in a strange way. He coughed. "I guess you'll be okay until we get back to the motel." He turned to Grandpa. "We really appreciate your help."

"Glad we had a chance to get acquainted." Grandpa said, "Would the two of you like to come back later and have supper with us?"

Claude said, "We'd be glad to share supper with you. All we've had the past few days is food from the diner in town."

Grandpa opened a cupboard and brought out his Last Chance Emergency Shoebox. He pushed aside the Bicentennial quarters he always saved. After counting out two five-dollar bills, he passed the cash over to me. "Here, take this to Popper's Market. Get me some heartburn medicine and milk. Buy a large can of beef stew. If there's enough money, bring back a box of those chocolate cookies with frosting in the middle. We'll be having a good supper tonight." Dipping into his last chance box was always Grandpa's way of saying things were certain to get better soon.

Claude took out his car keys. "Buddie, we can give you a lift into town. We're stopping for gas on our way back to the motel. Isn't the grocery store right across from the gas station?"

On the way into town with Claude and Wilbur, words from Lincoln's note came to mind. I wondered if most of the people in the world were poor folk hoping for a last chance in life.

Chapter Fourteen

Can This Day Get Any Worse?

I left Claude and Wilbur at the gas station across the street from Popper's Market. In less than ten minutes, I had the groceries Grandpa wanted at the checkout, but I couldn't get away from Mrs. Popper. As she rang up my groceries, she asked question after question about the vase.

"Who on earth do you think took Lutie's vase? Where did people like you get such a valuable antique anyway?"

I didn't care for her "people like you" remark, so keeping my mouth shut turned out to be easy. Anyway, her questions faded into the background because some kind of commotion started up over at the gas station. Men hurried across the street. A funny feeling came over me that whatever might be happening, Wilbur and Claude were involved. By the time I got away from Mrs. Popper and ran outside, a dozen men circled the gas pumps.

At the center of the circle, Mr. Webb stood in the back of his truck. He pointed to Claude and Wilbur while he made wild gestures with the stub of a cigar stuck between his fingers. His voice thundered. "We got to show these two skunks what we think of thieves."

Claude and Wilbur huddled between the truck and the gas pumps. I saw Johnny Watson, the station attendant, inside the office, frantically trying to dial the phone. Standing off to the front side of the truck, Keach watched her father and the two men. By easing my way around the front of the truck, I got to Keach without her father seeing me.

I tugged on her sleeve. "What's your pa up to?"

"We happened to be driving by and saw these crooks right here in broad daylight. They're likely gassing up to skip town. If we don't stop them now, they'll be gone forever."

Mr. Webb dropped his cigar stub onto the truck bed and ground it out with the heel of his boot. "These weasels got a lot of nerve," He shook his fist at Wilbur and Claude. "Strangers have no right coming in here stealing from us hard-working folks."

Most of the men in the crowd were farmers probably in town to buy feed and supplies. They wore caps with patches advertising "Pioneer Seeds" or "John Deere" sewed above the bills. Some watched with hands jammed in their pockets. One or two spat thin streams of chewing tobacco onto the cement.

"Where's the sheriff?" I asked, keeping my eyes peeled for signs of trouble in the crowd.

"Johnny said the sheriff is in Jasper until tonight." Keach stood with her hands on her hips. "We'll nab these thieves and make a citizen's arrest before they leave."

The steady, thoughtful farmers listening to Mr. Webb were not the kind of men to be easily upset. Between Mr. Webb's outbursts, waves of silence drifted like campfire smoke. Claude spotted me watching, and he raised his eyebrows as if pleading for help. Should I speak up, or did he need me to stay quiet and not blow what was left of their cover? A restless stirring rippled through the crowd, and a knot settled in my stomach. Handing my groceries to Keach, I gathered my courage and plunged ahead.

"Let them go!" Shoulders parted as I walked through the crowd and around to the back of the truck. "Grandpa and I know these men. They are not thieves."

Saul Webb's face darkened, but his words came out soft and patient as if he spoke to a three-year-old. "You're not feeling sorry for these drifters, are you, Buddie? After all, who else could have taken your vase? I bet Lutie never owned an antique more valuable than that beautiful crimson vase. Right?"

Without answering, I turned, stared into the crowd, and tried to look confident and adult.

"Listen to her," Claude begged. "Lutie will back us up. We're here on honest business."

Men dropped out of the circle and wandered away, making me thankful for Grandpa's good reputation.

"Wait a minute everybody!" Mr. Webb's voice grew louder, but power faded from his words. "You'll all be sorry you let these thieves get away!" I felt Mr. Webb glaring at the back of my neck, but I refused to turn and meet his gaze.

Keach walked around to where I stood and shoved the sack of groceries at me. "I can't believe you. We try to help, and you let them off the hook. You ruined our best chance to catch these thieves." Keach and her father climbed into their truck, slammed the doors, and sped away. I jumped sideways in time to miss being pelted with spitting gravel.

On a hilltop a safe distance from town, I looked back. Wilbur dropped some change in the gas station candy machine. Claude and Johnny Watson huddled close in conversation by the gas pumps. A tall boy hurried up the hill toward me. *Adam.* A bitter taste rose in my mouth. Still angry, I made up my mind to tell Adam what I thought of him and never speak to him again.

"Hey! Wait up. You're sure in a hurry to leave. I missed you at the farm."

Refusing to look at him, I walked even faster. "I was there."

"When? I waited all afternoon."

"You didn't see me behind the maple tree by the fence. You looked busy, so I left."

Adam picked up a pebble and threw it into brush beside the road. "Sure, I was busy. I had plenty of work. You might have come in and let me know you were there."

I stopped and faced him. "Courtney and you were by the water barrel. You didn't look like you needed company." With that, I hurried on and left him standing in the road.

Adam caught up with me and broke a twig from a dogwood tree by the road. Snapping the twig into bits, he dropped them one by one as we walked. "Courtney was supposed to be out of town. You know, every time I think we're done being friends, she gets all chummy again. One day she acts like she doesn't know me, and the next day she's a pest."

"You didn't look pestered when she dumped water all over you."

"I never know what to say or how to act. Anyway, if you're so shy, why did you speak up and save those strangers back there?"

"What was I supposed to do? Stay quiet and watch them get beat up?" I told him about the Everett farm and how Wilbur got chiggers.

Adam took the groceries from me and carried them. "Sorry I wasn't there for the sideshow with Wilbur and the chiggers."

We laughed, and any problem between us dissolved. *Maybe I'd keep talking to Adam after all.* "Claude and

Wilbur are really detectives looking for thieves who steal antiques."

"How do you know they are telling the truth about being detectives?"

"Grandpa believed them. He's pretty good at sizing people up."

"What if he's wrong? Anybody smart enough to steal antiques is smart enough to make up a good lie. Maybe they are thieves. Who else could have taken Lutie's vase?"

"Grandpa believes the thief knew Mrs. Nelson went to church every Sunday."

Adam nodded. "That's true. Wilbur and Claude were in town less than two days."

We stopped by the mailbox in front of my house. Neither of us came up with clues linking the vase to anyone other than Wilbur and Claude.

"You'd better stop worrying so much about the vase." Adam gave me back my groceries. "Go with me to the farm tomorrow. I'll stop by and we'll walk over together. There won't be many people working on a Wednesday afternoon."

"You mean Courtney won't be there?"

Adam nodded. "She always goes to Louisville for her dancing lesson on Wednesday. I'll stop by here right after lunch."

"If you'll walk with me, I'll go."

By the time I went inside the house, Grandpa had fallen asleep again in his wicker chair. His head lolled against the cushion, and his mouth hung open, releasing soft snores in a gentle rhythm. His hands held the latest sweepstakes entry open on his lap. In bold black print, the flyer once again promised we might be the grand prize winner. Did he dream about winning the sweepstakes? Grandpa sat with his legs stretched out and his feet bare. A stray piece of garlic had fallen between his toes.

I opened the can of stew I'd bought and turned the stove on low, letting the smell of warm food wake Grandpa slowly.

He woke and rubbed his eyes. Never one to waste anything, he picked up the fallen clove of garlic and dropped it into his overall pocket. As he pulled on his socks and shoes, Wilbur and Claude arrived. Claude helped me set the table. Wilbur stirred the stew while he took deep breaths of the steaming aroma.

When we sat to eat, Grandpa asked the blessing, and then, we dug in. I waited for Wilbur or Claude to bring up the trouble in town, but neither of them mentioned a word about Mr. Webb or the gas station. I bit my lip to keep from blabbing.

Claude entertained us with stories of other cases he had solved. Wilbur thanked us for the relief provided by the bath and calamine lotion while he finished off the last of the stew. Both men said supper was the best home-cooked meal they'd tasted in months.

After supper, I washed the dishes while Claude and Wilbur dried them. Then, we joined Grandpa in the living room. Claude paced back and forth. "Lutie, there is one other thing we need to talk about, but I didn't want to spoil dinner with unhappy news." Grandpa perked up and listened. For the next twenty minutes, Claude, Wilbur, and I filled in the details from the gas station.

Grandpa looked at me and smiled. "Good for you, Buddie. Let's celebrate." He stood, went to the kitchen counter, and opened the box of cookies. "Here's my favorite dessert." He offered the cookies to our guests and to me. He took two for himself and sat in his wicker chair.

Within a minute or two, Grandpa polished off his cookies. "The thing is, Saul Webb hasn't been in Whistler long enough to understand how people here think. We won't be stirred up by an angry man spouting off in public. What if Buddie and I keep spreading the word you're here on honest business? If we vouch for you, people will begin looking for the real thieves."

Claude settled back in his chair and stretched his arms. "We'd be grateful. With your help, Saul may be forced to leave us alone."

Awake in bed that night, I thought about my walk home with Adam. Remembering his words, I whispered to myself, "Courtney is a pest." I hugged my pillow, giggled in the dark, and drifted off to asleep. Around midnight, an image of Mr. Webb's face with snakes writhing in his hair and around his neck startled me from a deep sleep.

Chapter Fifteen

A Lofty Choice

Adam and I arrived at the farm the next day in time to see an older man adding rails to the fence. When the man paused in his work, Adam said, "Mr. Dawson, this is Buddie McBride. She wants to help us. I'm going to show her around."

Perspiration ran down the man's bald head, over his tanned face, and into a salt-and-pepper handlebar mustache. Mr. Dawson's ruddy complexion and stained brown apron reminded me of an old-time blacksmith. He wiped his hands on his apron. "Good. We need more volunteers. Do you know anything about pioneer life?"

"My grandpa and I make mandolins and banjos. He taught me some of the old songs."

"Oh, you're Lutie's granddaughter." He sounded a little impressed, and I appreciated him for recognizing Grandpa. "Look around. You'll find plenty of work. Several of us will be here all afternoon. Stay as little or as long as you like."

Adam had been right. Not many people were around, but lots of animals made the farm feel busy. Three sheep grazed beneath trees inside a large pen while chickens cackled behind a stockade fence. The tops of sharpened posts around the poultry yard kept chickens from perching on the fence. Inside another pen, a spotted cow stood heavily beside her spindly-legged, sand-colored calf. The calf nosed at a monarch butterfly clinging to a weed. The fluttering butterfly caused the calf to take a quick, stiff-legged jump backwards.

Adam waved his hand at the butterfly. "Do you think butterflies know how many miles it is to Mexico?"

"Even if the butterflies know, they won't care. Those tiny wings will keep flapping until nature takes them where they need to be."

"Adam! Buddie! Over here." Mr. Dawson motioned for us to join him beside a small barrel filled with ashes. A sloping trough connected the barrel with a large pottery crock. Mr. Dawson handed Adam a bucket. "Fill this bucket with water and pour the water into the small barrel."

Adam did as he was told. The water ran through the ashes in the barrel, down the trough, and emptied into the crock. I filled an extra bucket and between us we kept the water flowing.

Mr. Dawson took three eggs from a sack. "Keep pouring and add an egg from time to time. When the solution is strong enough, one of the eggs will float." He placed the eggs beside the crock. "Wear these gloves and goggles and be careful not to get any of the ash water on your skin or clothes."

"What's this going to be?" Adam asked as he refilled his bucket.

"We'll use the solution to make old-fashioned lye soap in a craft demonstration." Mr. Dawson turned to me. "Buddie, your grandfather works with wood. Does that mean you know how to whittle?"

"A little but nothing fancy. That's Grandpa's specialty."

"I may have another project for you." Mr. Dawson went into the tool shed and came back with a whittling knife and a dozen foot long sticks. "We need to carve these into pegs to hold the fence posts together." He handed me a finished peg. "So far, we've attached the rails with wire, but pioneers held their fences together with pegs. Once the pegs are in place, we'll be able to connect the rails without using any wire. That's what Abe would have done."

"These shouldn't be hard to make." I sat with my back against a tree and piled the sticks near my feet. As I whittled, now and then, I glanced at Adam pouring water through the trough.

Finally, when an egg did float, he whooped. He set the bucket on the ground and came to sit with me under the tree. The way he asked questions about how I held the wood and used the knife made my everyday whittling feel special.

I offered him the knife and a peg. "These are easy. Here, let me show you."

Adam made a couple of awkward slices. "Never mind. I'd rather watch you work." After I finished carving the last peg, he stood and offered me his hand. "Help me hang a few bunches of herbs in the cabin. Then, we'll go home."

Instead of glass, greased paper covering the cabin's single window made the interior dim and musty. A bed and a small, three-legged stool covered half the wall space in the one main room. A rough table with hand-hewn benches filled most of the floor space in front of the fireplace. Handmade beeswax candles, sacks of dried beans, and twists of tobacco hung from pegs pounded into the logs. Still, the cabin felt empty, as if needing people to add life.

Adam stood on a stool while I gave him bunches of lavender and lemon balm to hang from the rafters. "Can you believe nine people once lived in a cabin no bigger than this?" he asked as I gave him the last bunch of lavender.

"Lincoln's parents must have slept in the bed. Where did the kids sleep?"

Adam hopped off the stool and walked to the fireplace wall. He caught hold of long pegs sticking out between the fireplace stones. The pegs set one above the other made a ladder up to the loft.

"Why are the two bottom pegs wider apart than the higher ones?"

"Follow me. I'll show you."

Adam grabbed the higher of the two bottom pegs. "See? If the kids couldn't reach the second peg, the parents knew they were too little to sleep in the loft, but that's no problem for us."

He scrambled up the peg ladder, and I climbed after him.

The slope of the roof made standing possible only in the center of the loft. Without windows, the pitched roof trapped the heat, making the loft warmer than the room below. Two smoked hams hung from rafters, while three sleeping pallets with patchwork quilts covered the floor. I wondered what Abe Lincoln dreamed while sleeping on a pallet in a loft like this.

Adam waited and watched from the center of the room while I smoothed the quilts and sniffed the salty dried hams. When I walked back to the center of the loft, we faced each other not more than a foot apart.

"I think you like this place as much as I do," he said. "Are you glad we're here?"

"I love this cabin, and I'm happy we're hanging out again."

"Me too." He slid his arm around my waist and brought his face closer to mine.

In a flash, I knew Adam wasn't thinking about the quilts or the salty hams. His eyes shone, and small drops of moisture beaded above his lip. The scent of lavender clung to his black T-shirt. Outside in a nearby tree, a bird sang like freedom's call in the summer afternoon.

I think I smiled, maybe a little. Right before he kissed me, I ducked. His kiss landed on top of my head. I quickly moved away and looked back.

Adam smiled his half-crooked, awkward smile.

I smiled back at him. "You're almost as shy as I am, aren't you?"

His face turned red and he looked away. "About some things."

I didn't have time to think about why I ducked. Maybe our friendship made me happy enough, or maybe like the bird, I wanted to stay free to fly to other places. Later, I understood if a situation isn't comfortable, the word "no" doesn't need a reason.

We made our way back down the pegs. I took a final look around the main cabin. "Remember the other day you said this farm is a very interesting place? You sure were right."

Adam laughed.

We found Mr. Dawson in the tool shed and let him know we were leaving. Adam and I talked all the way home, but I can't remember what we said because the old ballad "Froggy Went A-Courtin'" kept running around inside my head.

Chapter Sixteen

KEACH'S DANGEROUS PLAN

For the next week and a half, Adam and I spent almost every day together. On Wednesdays, we worked at the Lincoln farm. On other days, he helped us finish the mandolin and banjo Grandpa planned to sell at the festival in Bean Blossom. We took turns with Adam polishing the wood on one while Grandpa and I added strings and worked on the tuning for the other.

Often, Adam went home for supper and came back later with his guitar. We sat together on the porch trading what he knew about the guitar with what I knew about the mandolin. Usually, we swapped instruments and played until Grandpa called me to come in for the night. Each time Adam left, I hoped to see him the next day. He always came back. Grandpa invited Adam to ride with us to the festival. As things turned out, his dad needed him to work in the field the same day we planned to ride with Miss Emily.

I hadn't seen Keach since my run-in with her dad at the gas station. Once or twice, I thought I heard her in the woods. She never came over, though, and I stayed too busy to get to her place. Anyway, she was the angry one. I'd wait until she cooled off and felt ready to patch up our friendship.

The day of the festival, Miss Emily came for us at six o'clock in the morning. Two and a half hours later, she let us off beside a long, low jamboree barn at Bill Monroe's farm. We bought tickets from a girl about my age wearing a yellow T-shirt with "Bean Blossom Bluegrass" printed on the front. I hoped we might have enough money at the end of the day to buy a shirt for me.

We picked our way across a field between every kind of rig–from pup tents to fancy Winnebagos sporting long antennas. A boy sitting on the back of a truck smiled at me while he tuned his fiddle. He tapped his boots against a bumper sticker with the words: "If you ate supper last night, thank a farmer." When he patted the truck bed next to him, Grandpa nodded his approval and walked on. I jumped up next to the fiddler. We ran through a few tunes together until a woman stuck her head out of a trailer parked nearby and called him to breakfast.

I joined the crowd streaming toward music coming from a grove of white-washed trees. Grandpa saved a seat for me on one of the narrow benches nailed between tree trunks. Our newly finished banjo and mandolin leaned against the oak tree next to me. Grandpa had placed a hand-lettered "For Sale" sign in front of them.

Lovers had left carved initials with hearts and arrows in the trunk of the oak. Tracing my fingers over the words, "Nathan loves Alice, forever," I wondered where Nathan and Alice were, and if their "forever" had already come and gone.

Three men tuned instruments on the crudely built wooden stage. The guitar player yelled, "How many people we got here today?"

A man near the stage hugged his pregnant wife and hollered back, "About a million, and soon to be a million plus one."

Before long, an old man with a shaved head hobbled over to us. He pointed to the sign in front of the banjo. "That yer banjo for sale?"

Grandpa picked up the banjo and offered it to him. "Do you play?"

"Used to. My good ol' banjo wore out before I did. Now I need one for my grandson. Mind if I give this one a try?"

Grandpa and the man walked off to talk music and money. He came back a few minutes later with money in his hand and no banjo as a new group bounded on stage. When the first song ended, I caught sight of Keach crossing a meadow on the far side of the trees.

I told Grandpa I'd be back.

He nodded and tucked the money from his sale into his overall pocket.

I ran off, passing by couples sitting on blankets near the edge of the trees. Most of them looked more interested in each other than in the music. A young man yelled, "Hey!" when I jumped across the end of his blanket.

"Watch out young'un!" A large woman on a bike wobbled until she swerved around me. A baby slept, oblivious, in the infant seat behind her.

A few minutes later, I spotted Keach again in front of a huge, forked maple. She spoke earnestly to a man wearing a plaid work shirt. I wondered why in this world she would be interested in talking to Clem Farney. I watched from a distance until Clem left.

As soon as Keach saw me, she waved and ran to meet me as if our trouble never happened.

"I hoped you would be here. I've been wanting to see you."

"Grandpa and I rode over with Miss Emily. Come sit with us."

Keach had combed her hair in a new style, down over one side of her face. She followed me without a word about what happened at the gas station. I was happy to leave our anger in the past. As soon as we sat, two brothers and their backup group came onstage.

During the applause Grandpa whispered into my right ear. "Look at Keach's face!"

Turning toward her, I saw what he meant. The hair she carefully pulled down over her right cheek slid back over her ear, revealing a faded bruise the size of a silver dollar.

I leaned over and asked Keach, "What happened to your face?"

Her hand flew up, and she hid the bruise. "Running through the woods the other day, I tried to get to your place and fell over a tree root. I ran back home and held an ice pack on my face right away. Even though this bruise looks awful, it never did hurt much."

Keach always talked too much when she tried to shade the truth. Grandpa listened to Keach, but he didn't say a word. I don't think he believed her, and neither did I.

When Bill Monroe and his Bluegrass Boys bounded on stage, Grandpa turned to us. "Watch and listen carefully, girls. Now you're going to see some style."

He liked to talk about what he called "style." Grandpa believed all great performers developed their own special way to capture an audience. According to him, style develops when performers care so much about their fans, they pour all of their heart and soul into their music.

We often watched Bill Monroe play at Bean Blossom. This time, I paid attention to how he interacted with the audience while I listened to some of the best picking in the country. For the first time, I saw what Grandpa meant by style. I knew why he had trouble describing what he called the "gift of all great performers."

The three of us spent the afternoon sitting in the grove of trees on our bench in front of the stage. We ate hot dogs, lost in the sound of first one band and then another. Late in the afternoon Keach and I wandered back to tables set up for performers to sell tapes and albums. Ma Lewis and her daughter Miggie of the famous Lewis Family hovered like mother hens over three tables full of albums and merchandise. Ma Lewis didn't seem to mind when we picked up a copy of every album and read the songs listed on the back.

After I returned one album to the table, Keach pulled me off to the side. "I'm leaving home, and I have to talk to you before I go."

The edge in her voice sent a chill through my stomach. I turned and faced her. "You mean you're leaving as soon as you save enough money?"

Keach shook her head, and we moved further away from the table area. "No. I'm going next week. Here's my perfect plan. Clem's catching a freight train south. I'm riding with him as far as Nashville."

"Nobody hops freight trains these days."

"Clem does."

"What will you do in Nashville?"

"Just listen. I'll get a job. Lots of bands need backup players."

"Keach, look around us. Nashville is full of pickers as good, or better, than anybody here. Why do you think they'll hire you?"

"Not just me. Us." She put a hand on my shoulder and smiled. "This is our chance. The two of us can get plenty of work. You need to come with me."

"No!" I shook my head. "I'm not ready to leave."

"I guess you're not much of a friend after all." She walked back to the merchandise tables and thumbed through the albums.

Still hoping to persuade her to stay, I joined her. "Don't you see? *Because* I am your friend, I won't go with you. What you're talking about is dangerous and probably illegal."

Keach sighed. "Living with my pa is dangerous too. My life has gone from bad to worse. Friends help friends. I need your help to get away."

"Did he give you that bruise on your face?"

Her eyes filled with tears. Before they spilled, Grandpa and a white-haired man wearing a shoestring necktie came toward us. Keach quickly rubbed the back of her hand across her eyes.

"Come talk to me after we get home, but don't be thinking I'll go with you. Grandpa will help find a way out of your problem."

The man with Grandpa carried our mandolin slung over his shoulder. They stopped in front of us. "Girls, meet my old friend, Whizzer Gilles. We go back a long way."

My face must have lit up because Whizzer smiled. "I bet you've heard Lutie speak of me."

"Yes, sir. He's told me how the two of you traveled all over, playing at county fairs."

Whizzer nodded toward the jamboree barn where musicians were gathering for an impromptu jam session. "Maybe you can join us for a little music."

"Can't stay this time," Grandpa motioned across the road to where Miss Emily waited beside her van. "Our ride is here to take us home."

"What about you, missy?" Whizzer offered me his new mandolin. "It'll do me good to hear Lutie's kin pick a bit of somethin' purty."

Playing a little was the least I could do since he bought our mandolin. After checking the tuning, I picked a crisp, sassy bit of "Foggy Mountain Breakdown." People heading toward the jamboree barn stopped to listen. Happy to have an audience, I played my best.

After the finish, Whizzer shook my hand and said to Grandpa, "You passed the gift on, old man. Your granddaughter does you proud."

"Stay safe, Whizzer," Grandpa slapped a hand on the man's shoulder. "We'll see you next time."

I hated missing the jam session in the barn, but Miss Emily waved at us from her van while she patiently waited in the parking lot.

Keach walked with me part way. Before turning back, she whispered, "Don't forget. I'll come and see you in a day or two." She edged past the barn where Mr. Webb stood talking with a rough looking bunch of men and slipped into her father's truck.

Grandpa watched the men for a moment. "You think Keach got that bruise tripping over a tree root?"

"I've never known her to stumble over roots before."

"That's what I thought." Grandpa walked toward Mr. Webb and called him aside. "What happened to Keach's face?"

"That girl," Mr. Webb shook his head. "She jumped off the back of the truck the other day and got the most awful bump."

"That so?" Grandpa raised one eyebrow. "She told us she stumbled over a tree root."

Keach slouched on the front seat of the truck.

"Don't matter how she got any little bruise." Mr. Webb's face turned red. "Kids get hurt. Whatever she did, she brought on herself. Anyway, best if you mind your own business."

"Your business is your business, but if she got hurt the way I think she did, that would be everybody's business."

Mr. Webb strode to his truck and jerked open the passenger door. "I don't care what she said. Ask her now. You'll see. My girl will back me up. Go on. Ask her."

Grandpa stood his ground. "I don't have to ask her. The truth is written all over her face."

"Kathrine, we're leaving." Mr. Webb put his hand on Keach's arm. "We'll eat supper and come back later to buy a bunch of those Lewis Family albums I saw you looking at this afternoon." He slammed the passenger door so hard Keach jumped in her seat.

As her father's truck sped away, Keach huddled like a cornered fox. I knew she'd leave home soon with or without any help from me.

Chapter Seventeen

An Emergency Detour

"We'll go for now." Grandpa guided me toward Miss Emily's van. "We need time to figure out how to deal with Saul Webb."

Miss Emily had half a dozen cardboard boxes in the back of her van.

Grandpa glanced at the few boxes of dishes. "You didn't buy much."

Miss Emily started the van and drove away from the festival. "Oh, their ads claimed they had lots of antiques, and they did. Most of them were in such bad shape they were worthless. I did find several pieces of carnival glass though. That's about all."

Sunset cast a golden glow over the countryside. We sped past hillsides covered with pink crown vetch and four white horses grazing in an emerald green meadow. While Grandpa dozed, I tried to figure out a way to keep Keach safe in Whistler. If Grandpa and I could spend time talking, we'd think of at least a couple of good ideas.

The two of us were hot and dusty before Miss Emily picked us up, but now the air conditioner in her van poured cool air around us. The chilly air made me feel clammy.

Grandpa startled me when he snorted and woke up. Sweat welled up in dark splotches on his shirt. Grandpa stared out the window as he told Miss Emily about the bruise on Keach's cheek and his talk with Mr. Webb. Between sentences, he paused to take small breaths.

"Emily ... the time has come to ... to do something ... about Saul Webb."

His voice sounded close to normal. I couldn't tell if he was in pain. Maybe the pauses were only to choose what to say next.

"Do you think Saul struck her?" Miss Emily glanced at Grandpa. then concentrated again on the road ahead.

"More than ... likely he did," Grandpa's voice rose and shook with anger.

"Buddie, do you know whether or not Saul has ever hit Keach?" Miss Emily asked.

"Before today? No. She doesn't like to be around him, but she never explains why."

"Then we have no proof. Buddie, you talk to her as soon as you can. She might tell you what's going on if she knows we're willing to help."

Grandpa's breath became a choking cough, and he rubbed his chest.

Miss Emily slowed the van and looked over at him. "Are you okay?"

"A little heartburn," he gasped. "Too many hot dogs."

Miss Emily swung the van into a rest area and stopped. She walked around to the passenger side and opened the door. "Lutie, I'm putting you in back so you can lie down and get some rest." The tone of her voice meant this was an order and not a request.

I waited for Grandpa to argue, but he climbed out gripping the side of the van. With white knuckled hands, he stood there shaking. I hopped out too and put my shoulder under one of his arms, while Miss Emily steered him toward the back door.

We helped him get comfortable on the plush, gray carpet between boxes of fragile iridescent glass in the rear of the van. "You'd better ride back here with him." Miss Emily pointed to the space beside Grandpa.

I climbed in and sat on the floor beside Grandpa, putting one hand on his arm. Miss Emily pulled onto the highway. As we hurtled along, I prayed we wouldn't hit any major potholes.

Soon, Grandpa breathed easier. In spite of the bumpy road, I managed to pull myself up and lean against the back of the front seat. We passed barns with gleaming silos and corn cribs in clumps about half a mile apart. In the long summer dusk, a sixty-foot-tall tulip poplar tree, branches alive on one side and dead on the other, cast an eerie shadow across the road.

As I watched Grandpa, his face changed from a deep tan to a bluish gray. I brushed damp white hair from his forehead, willing my touch to make him better. For the first time ever, I saw him as old—maybe older than the tulip poplar by the side of the road.

I glanced up in time to see the van headlights flicker on the Shannon Creek bridge sign. Miss Emily missed the turnoff for Whistler. Without asking, I guessed she meant to take us to Evansville, and I think I knew why.

The pinched expression on Grandpa's face softened. I stood and tapped Miss Emily's shoulder. "Let's go home. He's getting better. I'm sure he'll be okay." My voice must have triggered a glimmer of recognition in Grandpa. His eyes opened, glassy at first, then he saw me.

"Didn't mean to scare you," His voice sounded weak and far away.

I wanted to hug him close but settled for kneeling and squeezing his hand. Miss Emily didn't look back at the sound of his voice. In fact, she drove faster.

"Tell her to take me home." His voice crackled like dry autumn leaves.

I leaned over Miss Emily's shoulder. "Grandpa wants to go home. Maybe that's what we ought to do. He knows what he needs."

She shook her head and stared straight ahead. "We'll soon be at the hospital. Just to be on the safe side, the doctor can look him over. Then we'll all go home together."

I sat on the floor next to Grandpa. He focused on my face and there was an urgency in his voice. "You know that doctor will charge plenty to take a look at me, don't you?"

I knew, but didn't want to think about money. "Have you ever won an argument with Miss Emily?"

He sighed deeply and turned his face the other way.

Before long, we arrived at the hospital emergency entrance. Miss Emily opened her door and looked back at me. "Stay here. I'll get an attendant with a wheelchair."

At the word wheelchair, Grandpa sat up. "Enough is enough, Emily." He struggled to his feet. "At least I can go in under my own steam."

Even with Grandpa's effort, we still had to help him out of the van. With each small step toward the emergency room entrance, he winced. Marigolds bloomed in large stone urns on either side of the emergency room door. He stopped and plucked one of the blossoms. Twirling the golden flower close to his face, he studied the petals. With another step, the automatic door opened. Cool air rushed out, blowing a powerful antiseptic smell in our faces.

Miss Emily waved at a nurse and pointed to Grandpa. "Chest pains."

An attendant wheeled a gurney over and took charge. We heard Grandpa wheezing even after they pushed him into a side room and closed the door.

While we answered the desk clerk's questions, Miss Emily surprised me with how much she knew about Grandpa's personal information.

The clerk asked for a contact phone number. Miss Emily offered the young woman one of her business cards. "Here's the number of my shop during the day." She also handed the clerk a slip of paper— "This is Sheriff Freeman's number in Whistler. Call him if you can't get in touch with me."

After that, we had nothing to do but wait. I picked up the marigold Grandpa let fall on the floor and sat on a green, plastic-covered, padded chair. Bits of stuffing bulged through a tear in the plastic covering the armrest. I pulled out little wisps of stuffing from the rip in the plastic while I wondered how soon we could go home. I pushed the stem of the marigold into the rip, as if planting the flower in the armrest might send fresh life through the plucked stem.

Nurses and doctors hurried in and out of Grandpa's room. Once, before the door closed, I caught a glimpse of his hand waving the nurses away. That tiny bit of motion made me feel better than watching people hurry in and out.

I wondered what would happen to me if they kept Grandpa in the hospital. Miss Emily seemed to read my mind. "I'll be staying with you, if the doctor decides to keep him here."

"You don't think he's coming home with us, do you?"

Miss Emily sat in the chair across from me. Now, she leaned closer. "I think they might want to run tests. He'll likely be here for a couple of days until they get the results back."

"You know that's exactly what he does not want. If you'd have taken us home, he would be fine. Grandpa knows how to take care of himself. He always gets better."

"Buddie," she spread her palms out to me. "Can't you see? Lutie needs help. He's probably needed medical care for a long time."

I stared at the ceiling made of white squares joined in large blocks. Nine smaller squares made up each large block. The ceiling lined up fifteen large blocks wide and eighteen blocks long. I almost figured out how many small squares were in the entire ceiling when a physician in a white coat came out of Grandpa's room. Miss Emily and I both stood.

"I'm Doctor Will Thomas. Are you relatives of Mr. McBride?"

"I'm his granddaughter." I waited, wanting yet not wanting, to hear what he had to say.

"Your grandfather had a heart attack."

Miss Emily put her arm around my shoulders.

Dr. Thomas spoke more to her than to me. "He is stable, but his situation is serious. You can see him now, but the medication we've given him will make conversation difficult. In a day or two, we'll know more about his condition." The doctor paused a moment as if to gauge our reaction to this news before he continued. "Why don't you visit for a few minutes, then go home and keep in touch by phone. We'll call as soon as we have test results. You'll also get a call from us if anything changes."

Miss Emily walked beside me with her hand on my back. Grandpa looked as if he had withered beneath the sheets. He reminded me of a pile of sticks—like the kindling we tossed in the wood stove. Wires connected him to machines all over the place. I sat on a chair by his bed and Miss Emily took the chair in the corner.

"Grandpa? It's me, Buddie. I'm here."

His eyelids opened, glassy at first as if he knew or tried to know, but he didn't respond.

As I reached out to touch him, the antiseptic hospital smell made me gag. I ran out and waited for Miss Emily to come and take me home.

Neither of us talked much all the way back to Whistler. The only thought I had was *please, God, please*, which I hoped counted as a prayer. Miss Emily stopped at her place and packed a few things in an overnight bag. My stomach had a queasy feeling because I knew Grandpa wouldn't be inside our house waiting for me.

Later, sitting on the edge of my bed in the dark, I called to mind the sound of his saw cutting wood for instruments in the front room. Traces of the harsh scent of a piece of oak he'd cut the week before still lingered in the air. For a minute, I wondered if I called his name, would I hear him stomping his work boots on the back porch? I whispered, "Grandpa?"

Nobody answered.

Chapter Eighteen

A Troubling Opportunity

The next morning, I asked Miss Emily, "Can we go back to the hospital today?"

"Maybe. She straightened her hat. "As soon as we get back from church, I'll call to see how Lutie's doing. Even though today is Sunday, they might send him home if he's better."

I sat with Miss Emily in church. Afterward, we drove to her place where she called the hospital. There had been no change in Grandpa's condition, though, and the doctor had ordered more tests.

At breakfast Monday morning, Miss Emily cooked bacon, eggs, and toast she'd brought from her house the day before. "We'll drive down to the hospital today. If we show up, they will probably let us see him, regardless of his condition."

I pushed my eggs around the plate and thought before I spoke. "I've changed my mind. I don't want to go back until he's able to come home."

"Why?"

"I want to go, but what if he hasn't changed since we saw him? He looked terrible, and he didn't even know me.

I couldn't help him." I couldn't bring myself to ask, *What if he never gets better?*

"I know how hard it might be to see him the way he is now." Miss Emily offered me more bacon. "You need to understand, though, the dread you feel will increase the longer you wait to go back. We can drive down tomorrow, but on Wednesday, I'll be at the auction for Granny Witherspoon. She's been in that house of hers more than seventy years. Her antiques are prizes I can't pass up. I've got out-of-town customers coming Thursday. Of course, if the doctor says Lutie can come home, or if the hospital lets us know he is worse, we'll go at a moment's notice, no matter what."

Suddenly, I no longer felt hungry, and I pushed my plate away. "If the hospital doesn't call us to bring him home sooner, Friday might be the best day to go. By then, I really believe he will be lots better."

Miss Emily took our plates to the sink, then she stood there looking out the back window. Without turning around, she said, "We'll go when you're ready. Of course, the best news will be if they call for us to bring him home before Friday. That's what we'll pray for."

I stayed in the kitchen drying the dishes while Miss Emily got ready to leave for work. She stopped at the kitchen door before she left. "I'll phone the hospital as soon as I get to the shop."

After she left, I went out to weed the flower beds and vegetable garden before the day got too hot. After all, when Grandpa came home, a weed-free garden would bring a smile to his face. He had hooked up the garden hose and soaked the flowers and vegetable plants before we left for the festival. Now the beans and the last of the lettuce were wilting. So, I drenched the vegetables and then the flowers before I began pulling weeds.

Keach showed up and waited at the end of one row while I pulled the last few weeds out of the beans. She yanked up a piece of hawkweed and added it to the pile. “Miss Emily spread the word about Lutie. How is he?”

I tried to tell her, but no words came. Instead, hot tears spilled down my cheeks, and I couldn’t stop crying. Keach steered me toward the front porch. We sat in the rocking chairs for a long time until I wiped my eyes.

“I don’t know what’s going to happen to Grandpa or me. Not knowing scares me the most.” My voice sounded husky. I wished I had a glass of ice-cold sweet tea.

Keach pushed a toe against the porch floor, setting her rocker into motion. “I know. Ma got so sick before she died. Looking at her poor, sad face scared me. I watched her get sicker and sicker, fearing one day she wouldn’t be there. That’s exactly what happened.”

Keach’s words did not help me at all. “I want to see him, but what if I go and he’s worse?”

“Maybe I can help. I’m leaving town with Clem before dawn Thursday morning. We have to switch trains in Evansville. Come with us. We’ll go see Lutie. If he’s not better, you can ride with me to Nashville. If he is better, and you want to catch a bus back here, that’s fine, too.”

The unwelcome idea Grandpa might not get better stuck in my thoughts. I tried to hang onto a mental image of us walking in the woods, laughing while he chewed garlic.

“How will you get money to go to Nashville?”

“Pa’s driving to Louisville Wednesday night after Granny Witherspoon’s auction. He won’t get back until Friday. He keeps his bedroom door locked because he has cash in there. I know where he hides the key.” She paused and looked down the road in the direction of her house. "After he leaves, I'll get in and take a little. I won't need much—maybe fifty dollars. He owes me at least fifty and then some for all the cooking and cleaning I've done for him, and for other things too." Her hand touched the faded bruise on her cheek.

"He did that to your face, didn't he?"

"Yeah." She dropped her hand into her lap.

"Why?"

"I don't know. The evening after the trouble at the gas station, he hit me with his fist. He claimed I ought to have stopped you. He blamed me for those two men getting away."

A knot of anger rose in my chest. "Why didn't you tell us?"

"I nearly did, but then I got to thinking. What if I told and nobody believed me? My word against his? Who are they gonna believe?" She sighed. "If people start asking questions, Pa will kill me for sure. After all, he's all I got. Who'd stop him?"

"Has he ever hit you before the day at the gas station?"

She shook her head. "Not before the gas station and not since, but his words hurt as bad as his fists. Last few weeks, he blames me for everything. He blamed me for Lutie asking questions at the festival. He even told me I'm the reason we didn't win first prize at the talent contest." She looked at me with deep sadness in her eyes. "Is that true, Buddie? Was I the reason we didn't win first prize?"

"Of course not. We didn't win because Adam is a great guitar player. He won because he deserved first prize." I gave her an honest answer, and she looked relieved.

"I have to get away, and you need to see Lutie. Both of us will be better off if we travel together, at least as far as Evansville."

My head ached. By the time Keach finished talking, her plan made some kind of crazy sense. "I'll go with you as far as Evansville. After I see Grandpa, I'm coming home." A monarch butterfly hovered over Grandpa's pot of parsley and looked straight at me as if to say, *Buddie, are you traveling in the right direction?*

"Thanks, you'll be glad you listened to me." Keach smiled. "I know Adam's been over here all the time lately, but you're the best friend I've ever had. I saw Courtney's cousin in town last week. She told me Courtney is jealous, and she wants to get even with you. Courtney says the only reason Adam is over here is because of your music. She says otherwise, he wouldn't look twice at you."

"Courtney is jealous of me?" I laughed out loud and clapped my hands. "In the first place, she broke up with Adam. I don't know why she wants him back now." The butterfly settled on the parsley and didn't move. "Adam and I think alike about a lot of things. Leaving town means leaving Adam. Why would I do that?"

Keach stood and paced back and forth. "If Lutie is getting better, I might come back here with you. If he's worse, you'll have to think about what's going to happen to you here without him. Don't you know? A social worker will take you away and put you in a foster home, most likely in another county. You'll never see Adam again."

I hadn't thought about what might happen to me if Grandpa didn't get better. Miss Emily said she would stay until he came home. She did not promise to stay forever. The uncertainty made me desperate to see Grandpa.

"I don't have a lot of money. Grandpa sold the mandolin and banjo we took to Bean Blossom. Miss Emily thinks the hospital will keep the money he brought with him until he is released."

"Your house is full of stuff. What's the most valuable thing you have here?"

"We have an old rifle."

"That's good. The auction house can easily include your rifle in Granny Witherspoon's sale on Wednesday."

"You're beginning to remind me of your pa." I closed my eyes. "What if I don't want to sell Grandpa's rifle?"

"You can go right on sitting here doing nothing for Lutie or yourself. When your life falls apart, you'll have nobody to blame but yourself."

"Grandpa once told me if anything happened to him, whatever he owned would be mine. Now that he's in the hospital, I need money to be there for him. Come in and I'll show you the rifle." As we left the porch to go into the house, the butterfly on the parsley flew away. Once inside the house, I took the rifle from my closet shelf.

Keach ran her hand over the barrel. "Great, but let's not bother telling Miss Emily about what we're doing. She's already helped you enough."

The secret of Lincoln's cave hung heavy in my heart. Not telling Miss Emily I planned to leave made my burden of secrets even heavier. We took the rifle to the auction barn that afternoon. I told the auctioneer about Grandpa in the hospital and how I needed to sell the rifle.

The auctioneer studied the rifle and bit his lower lip as if he wondered what he should do. "This is a beautiful piece, but I can't help you unless somebody over eighteen signs the sale papers." So, we walked back into town and paid Miss Emily a visit after all.

Miss Emily listened carefully as she studied the rifle. "Lutie told me he had an antique rifle. I can see you'll rest easier if you have cash on hand. I'll sign the papers." Then she told me something Grandpa had never mentioned.

"Years ago, I signed a bunch of other papers for Lutie. If anything happens to him, those papers give me the right to see to your care. If anybody has the power to sign these sale papers, I do."

I avoided looking Miss Emily in the eye. She wouldn't understand how much I needed to see Grandpa before Friday. We took the rifle and papers back to the auction barn. On the way home, we agreed not to see each other until we met Clem in the train yard at five o'clock Thursday morning.

Earlier that day, I'd noticed a few strawberries, beans, and lettuce in the garden ready to be picked. At home, I found Adam waiting on the front porch. I motioned for him to follow as I headed for the garden.

"After we heard about Lutie, I wanted to see you." Adam sat down between two rows of ripe strawberries. "Mom told me to give you a little time before I came over."

I grabbed a basket we kept near the garden and began tossing in the ripe berries.

Adam popped a huge berry in his mouth. "How is Lutie?"

"When Miss Emily called the hospital this morning, the nurse said he's 'serious but stable,' whatever that means. Miss Emily is staying with me until he comes home."

Adam plucked another huge berry. "I'm helping you pick these." He popped the whole thing into his mouth.

"Picked berries go into my basket and not into your mouth."

Adam ignored me. Gathering three more berries, he opened his mouth and tossed them in. "These taste so good," he mumbled with his mouth full. "You'd better ask me to stay for supper before I eat all of them right here."

"Then stay." I wanted his company more than anything. We gathered the beans and lettuce and brought them into the kitchen. I opened a can of hash. The lettuce, beans, and berries were on the table by the time Miss Emily came home.

We sat at the table, and Miss Emily offered the blessing. She helped herself to the beans and passed the bowl to Adam. "This is a lovely surprise. I can't remember the last time anyone cooked supper for me." She passed the dish of hash. "So, Adam, what's going on at your farm?"

"Lately, Dad's given up on raising hogs. He tries to raise them for meat, but when butchering time comes, Mom doesn't have the heart to let him turn them into bacon. She says each one of those sweet pigs reminds her of one of Dad's relatives. She can't bear taking a bite out of any bacon reminding her of Uncle Willie or Aunt Lucy. Last year, we fed six hogs and bought all our bacon at the grocery store."

We laughed while Adam chewed with his mouth closed and ate berries with a spoon, instead of popping them into his mouth with his fingers.

Miss Emily talked about how strong Grandpa was for his age and how she expected him to come home any day. The three of us were having such a good time, I thought about what life might be like in the far future if Adam and I were more than friends. *What if we got married?* We'd have Miss Emily stop by now and then to eat supper. I'd have cloth napkins and plates that matched.

After Adam and I finished the dishes, we sat on the front porch. Miss Emily stayed in Grandpa's chair in the front room and read a book about Victorian furniture. The honeysuckle vine spilled perfume with wild freedom in the evening air. Crickets chirped and small animals made night noises in the brush. The sound of a truck shifting gears on the highway drifted across the fields.

Adam took my hand. "Want to go for a walk?"

I agreed, and we watched the sky turn crimson above the setting sun. Walking a little way toward town, we talked about everything and nothing. Then, in a moment without thinking, I spilled the beans about selling the rifle and traveling as far south as Evansville with Keach.

Adam stopped in the middle of the road. "That's got to be the dumbest idea I've ever heard. Let Miss Emily take you. People get hurt bad or even killed hitching trains."

I shook my head. "I won't take any more of Miss Emily's help. Grandpa wanted to come home, but she didn't listen. Besides, Keach's life with her dad is unbearable. She's counting on my help to get out of here. After I see Grandpa, I'll use the rifle money to catch a bus home."

"If Keach can talk you into hopping a train, she'll get you as far as Evansville and convince you to go on to Nashville." He turned and took long strides back toward the house while I ran to keep up. Before he left me standing in the yard, he took me by the shoulders. "I'm sorry you're leaving, but if you go with Keach, you'll be a lot sorrier than I am."

Chapter Nineteen

Miss Emily Fights Back

Wednesday morning, I arrived at the auction in time to see a dozen farmers milling around bins of tools while they waited for the bidding to begin. Several men picked through boxes of motors and spare parts as if hoping to find useful pieces to buy for bargain prices.

In the front yard, a harried mother in faded jeans changed her baby's diaper on Granny Witherspoon's old parlor loveseat. Young husbands and wives rummaged through boxes of table lamps, pots, and dishes. Now and then, an antique dealer eyed a handcrafted chair or table.

Granny Witherspoon sat in a lawn chair beneath her backyard apple tree. She surveyed the gathering crowd, and her shoulders slumped. Her face wore a look of resignation as strangers gathered to cart away the everyday fabric of her life. I thought about the Lincoln family and the household goods they left behind. Did life always come down to people having to choose between being tied down by what they owned, or letting go of possessions and moving on? After all, wasn't that the choice the Lincolns faced?

Grandpa and I often went to auctions. The auctioneer always sold off the junk first and saved the best antiques until the end. Lincoln's rifle gleamed behind the locked glass door of a tall cherry wood cabinet with no shelves inside. The rifle would be sold with the nicer antiques after lunch. I pressed my nose to the cabinet door and fought the urge to smash the glass, grab the rifle, and run back home.

Adam walked up beside me. "That the rifle you're selling?" He didn't sound angry, but I felt as if an invisible fence separated us.

"I'll own it until a bidder buys it after lunch. Grandpa told me this rifle is a 1795 Springfield flintlock musket."

Did Adam wonder if I changed my mind about leaving? He never asked. I think if he asked, I would have broken my promise to Keach and stayed. I changed the subject. "Are you here to buy or sell?"

Adam leaned against the cabinet. "I'm here with my dad. He wants to get a few pieces of machinery. Some of his old stuff is nearly shot, and new equipment costs too much. This past spring, Dad leased another fifty acres. He needs better machinery to farm the extra land."

"What do you mean he leased fifty acres?"

"A lease is like rent. He rented the acreage for the next five years. Each year, he pays for the use of the land after he sells the crop."

At that moment, Courtney stepped from behind the cabinet, and I jumped. I never imagined she might show up at the auction.

"Oh, Adam! How nice to see you here, and you too, Buddie." Her words spilled over us like sour milk from a broken jug. She grinned.

I did not say, "Nice to see you too."

"This must be my lucky day," Adam looked at neither of us.

Courtney stood a bit too close to Adam for my comfort. "My mom's here to buy Granny's bedroom furniture. Mom says the bed alone is worth at least a thousand dollars, but she thinks she can buy the whole set for three or four hundred. What are you here to buy, Buddie?"

"Nothing."

The lump stuck in my throat all morning grew larger. Nearby, the auctioneer jumped on a wagon bed filled with junk from the barn.

"Lookie here!" the auctioneer boomed through his microphone. "I've got a bucket with one little hole in the bottom. Let's start off on this one. Two, two, who'll gimme two dollars?"

No one raised a hand or even an eyebrow to offer a bid.

"How about a dollar? Everybody can use a bucket for a buck." The crowd stared blankly at the auctioneer. In a final effort he pleaded, "Okay, lemme have fifty cents!"

A thin man with a brace on one leg leaned on a carved walking stick and touched his cap.

The auctioneer chuckled and gave him the bucket. "It's yours, John Geiger, for fifty cents. Ol' John, I'm mighty pleased to see you here today."

John's mouth opened in a silent, toothless grin.

His wife beamed up at him from beneath her straw hat. "You're an old pack rat, you are." She spoke with a hint of girlish tease, and John handed her the bucket. She turned the bucket over and set it on the ground. The tiny woman bowed to her audience and perched on the upturned bucket. Onlookers applauded.

"There!" John pointed proudly at his wife. "See how useful a bucket can be?"

Turning to Adam, I asked, "Why does John buy worthless stuff like that?"

Courtney answered, "He doesn't keep any of the junk he buys. Wait here and watch. I'll show you what happens."

She walked to where John leaned patiently on his walking stick, waiting for the next item no one wanted. "Say, Mr. Geiger, what are you going to do with that old bucket?"

"Matter of fact, a bucket with a hole is full of possibilities. A one-hole bucket is handy for gathering eggs, or the missus might turn this one into a flower planter." He squinted at Courtney. "You want to buy this bucket from me for your mama? Price is only one dollar."

Courtney put her hands on her hips and shook her head. "Why, Mr. Geiger, not more than two minutes ago, I saw you give fifty cents for that bucket."

"True enough, but that was before folks knew the value of a bucket with a hole. Now that people see the value, the price has increased."

"What people are you talking about?" Courtney asked.

"Folks like you, young lady." He tipped his cap to Courtney.

"Not today, Mr. Geiger." She turned her back on the old man and walked toward us. "Don't you see? He sells all the junk he buys to suckers who give him more than he paid."

"Seventy cents! Seventy cents! That's my final offer," John called after her.

Adam shook his head and backed away. "You didn't need to do that." He looked at both of us. "The two of you are alike because I never know what to expect from either one of you." Adam left us standing there. I watched as he walked toward the barn and joined a group of farmers waiting to bid on machinery.

Adam's words stung, and tears welled up in my eyes. Even worse than selling the rifle, now I'd lost Adam's friendship. Right then I felt about as bad as when I was seven and got stuck in an outhouse at the town picnic.

Courtney pouted a little. “Wonder what’s gotten into him?”

“Courtney! Cooooourtney!” Her mother’s voice rang above the crowd. “Yoo-hoo! Courtney,” Cee Cee called, getting closer.

Did Courtney know how lucky she was to have a mama who always came looking for her? Instead of answering her mother, Courtney spotted our classmate, Butch Weems. She ran over to Butch and latched her elbow around his arm. They walked off together.

I wandered away from the bidding and found two girls selling hot dogs and pop from the back of a truck. Bottles of grape and orange pop bobbed in a water-filled zinc tub. The murky water sloshing around the bottles must have started out as ice earlier in the day. I used a little of my talent show money to buy a bottle of grape Nehi soda pop.

One of the girls pulled a dripping bottle from the tub. “How about a cold hot dog to go with this warm drink to even things up?”

I don’t know why, but I agreed. Away from the crowd, I sat in a shady spot under an oak tree. With sips of grape soda between bites, I managed to eat most of the hot dog. Nearby, a bunch of kids circled up to play a game.

The oldest girl said, “Let’s throw off all our shoes and count our toes.”

Sandals and tennis shoes flew. A dirty red sandal landed on my hand holding the last bite of hot dog. I wrinkled my nose at a little clump of dirt stuck on the bun and threw the last bite in a nearby garbage can, I moved to the other side of the tree and watched Adam help his dad load machinery onto their truck.

A few minutes after Adam left with his dad, Mr. Webb parked in their space. Almost immediately, Claude and

Wilbur drove into the field and found a parking spot. They climbed out of the VW and looked about as if searching for someone. Soon, the two men separated and disappeared into the crowd. I hurried to rejoin the bidding before anyone spotted me sitting alone under the tree.

Not long afterward, the auctioneer leapt onto the farmhouse porch and held Lincoln's rifle over his head. My heart raced when the bid rose from one to two hundred dollars. The bidding quickly climbed to four hundred. After a bid for six hundred, bidders paused while they considered whether to go higher or drop out. Then, a man in the back of the crowd waved his hand for six hundred and fifty dollars. The lump in my throat tightened when I realized the new bid came from Saul Webb.

"Lemme have a nice round sum," the auctioneer yelled. "Seven hundred, gimme seven!"

Mr. Dawson from the 4-H farm stood below the porch. He had bid six hundred. This time, he slowly shook his head.

The auctioneer bent down, coaxing while he spoke. "You're not going to let this all-original flintlock rifle get away for a few dollars more, are you?" He turned the old rifle slowly so that sunlight gleamed on the barrel.

Again Mr. Dawson shook his head and moved away.

"I'll go seven hundred!" a woman's voice shouted.

I turned to see Miss Emily waving her bidding paddle.

"Want to bid seven-fifty?" the auctioneer asked, nodding to Mr. Webb.

He agreed, and Miss Emily quickly added another fifty dollars to his bid. In fact, she topped every bid Mr. Webb made with another fifty. When the price soared to a thousand, Saul Webb exploded. "Emily! You know you'll never find a buyer willing to pay more than a thousand. If I go twelve hundred, you'll top that too, won't you?"

"You can try me and find out, or you can give in gracefully right now. Otherwise, when we get up around fifteen hundred, I'll drop out. Then that rifle will be your problem, not mine." She smiled, clearly enjoying her game of cat and mouse.

At that moment, I remembered Grandpa saying people wouldn't care about the Lincoln family or their treasures. He knew each piece would be valued purely for money. Even before the rifle could be sold, his words were coming true. I elbowed my way through the crowd, reached up to the porch, and tugged on the auctioneer's sleeve. He turned off his microphone and bent down. I looked him squarely in the face. "I've changed my mind."

He looked puzzled. "Don't do that. You're getting top dollar." I set my jaw and stared back at him until he pulled out his handkerchief and mopped his face. "Let's see what I can do."

He stood and turned on his microphone. "We have an unusual situation. The owner wants to withdraw her rifle from the sale. You're the high bid, Emily. What do you say? Will you drop your bid?"

She looked at Mr. Webb. "I'll drop the bidding if he will." She glanced my way and gave me the smallest wink.

Mr. Webb shrugged. He seemed a little relieved to be let off the hook, but he thundered back at Miss Emily. "This ain't over yet."

"Oh, I think we're done here, Saul." Miss Emily spoke with the same calm, firm tone of voice she used when she told students to sit down and be quiet.

As Mr. Webb stormed off, the anger that darkened his face made me shiver.

The auctioneer returned my rifle, with a word of caution. "Don't ever do that at an auction again."

He didn't sound angry, but I knew I'd not be trying to sell Lincoln's antiques again anytime soon. The auctioneer quickly began the bidding on an old pine table, and I moved away. Claude, Wilbur, Mr. Dawson, and Miss Emily followed me to get a better look at the rifle.

Claude ran his hand over the barrel. "This is the same rifle your grandpa brought to the farm. I've never seen one this old."

Miss Emily hugged me. "I am so glad you are keeping this. You did the right thing."

"Thanks for bidding against Mr. Webb." My words of appreciation were smaller than the gratitude in my heart.

"I would have given every penny to keep this rifle out of Saul's hands. Now that you have the rifle back, I'll be able to bid on the furniture being sold later."

"Mind if I see that for a minute?" Mr. Dawson braced the rifle against his shoulder and peered down the barrel. "Too bad I couldn't keep up with the bidding. Abe Lincoln might have owned a similar rifle. Just imagine this hanging over the cabin fireplace."

I swallowed hard, wondering if he guessed my secret. When he asked if I needed a ride home, I accepted, happy for the chance to get away.

Chapter Twenty

Trapped Like a Rabbit

Back in my bedroom, I realized the safest place for the rifle and Lincoln's note would be the trunk in the cave. Later that same afternoon, I wrapped the rifle in an old burlap sack, and dug out the metal box from under my bed. After memorizing Abe's words, I replaced the dingy paper and wrapped a piece of cloth around the box. I grabbed the rifle, metal box, and a small flashlight, and started down the path toward the gulley.

Except for our spring-fed creek, the land stood parched. Puffs of dust rose with every step. If rain didn't come soon, Adam's dad might be sorry he had leased those extra acres.

Crawling into the cave alone gave me goosebumps. The hollow beneath the earth made an echo chamber magnifying the sound of each falling pebble and scurrying insect. My flashlight danced spooky shadows on the back wall. I quickly hid the rifle and metal box inside the trunk and scrambled out.

In the late afternoon sunlight outside the cave entrance, I peered down into the gulley expecting to see nothing out of the ordinary. As my eyes adjusted to the light, I realized the trap door over the moonshine hideout had been moved to one side. Small cardboard boxes rose in stacks next to the opening. When a large form climbed out of the moonshine hole, I stifled a scream. The shape in the gulley belonged to a man, squatting and gathering the boxes in a sack. The moment I recognized Mr. Webb, our eyes locked. His face echoed the shock on mine.

"You!" he roared, dropping the sack into the hole.

Numb with fear, I watched as he scrambled across the gulley and pulled his way up the embankment.

When his head pushed over the gulley rim, he bellowed, "Stay there!"

I shoved my little flashlight into my pocket and ran for home. Mr. Webb's legs were longer than mine, but I knew every twist and turn in those woods. He plunged after me, cursing with every step, while his boots crashed through the brush.

The creek loomed fifty feet ahead with banks spread wide apart, making for a tricky jump. Between the steep sides, water a few inches deep gurgled over pebbles on the bottom. I glimpsed Mr. Webb closing in behind me. As his thick arms reached out, I jumped and stretched, grabbing for the weeds on the far side. The weeds held for a moment, then gave way, sending me backward into the water.

Mr. Webb leaped into the water, grabbed my ankle, and bellowed, "Gotcha!"

He yelped when I threw a handful of mud and pebbles in his face. We slid about in the stream until, in a moment when his fingers loosened, I jerked free and scrambled up the bank.

"Worthless brat!" He snorted, pulling himself out. "I'll skin you alive before dark." He pounded after me.

Beyond the trees not far ahead, home and safety beckoned. Then I remembered. We had never replaced the broken back door lock.

Out of breath, I scrambled inside and slammed the door. He banged the door open and stumbled after me. Filthy, smelling like mud scraped from the bottom of a stagnant pond, eyes bulging like a mad dog, Mr. Webb followed me through the kitchen and into the front room. He looked about, paused and picked up the half-finished neck of a banjo. Tapping the wood softly against his palm he grunted. "This'll do."

I reached for the front door but fell over tools scattered on the floor. Time slowed as Mr. Webb crept closer. Crazy things popped into my head, like the memory of a rabbit I once found caught in one of our traps. Grandpa explained the rabbit died, not from injury, but from the pure fright of being caught. With Mr. Webb now a few feet away, I knew the rabbit's terror.

What could I offer him to let me go? He couldn't hurt Grandpa. I ruined my friendship with Adam. Lincoln's belongings were safe in the trunk in the cave. When I realized I had nothing left to lose, perfect peace settled over me like a warm blanket.

I looked up at Mr. Webb and smiled. "Take anything you want."

"What?" He stopped, as stunned as if I'd struck the first blow.

"Look around. Whatever you want is yours."

Confusion clouded his face.

I stood and brushed off my clothes. "Help yourself. Take everything if that will make you happy."

He glanced toward Grandpa's bedroom.

"Guess you don't want this," I lifted my mandolin from a hook, eased out the front door, and collapsed in the rocking chair at the far end of the porch. If he came out after me, I planned to jump over the railing and run for town. I tried playing a little, but my hands shook so hard I couldn't pick a single note.

Meanwhile, I heard Mr. Webb rummaging around inside, knocking things over and banging drawers open and shut. A few minutes later, he opened the screen door. I stood, ready to hop the railing and run. He shook his fist toward me. "Stay away from me and my girl. If I catch you in the woods again, you'll see the saddest day of your life." He stormed back through the house, out the kitchen door, and into the woods.

When Miss Emily came home half an hour later, she found me still sitting in the rocking chair trying to play. She stared and asked gently, "What happened to you?"

"I ran into Mr. Webb in the woods. He chased me and I fell in the creek. Guess he's still hot under the collar about the rifle. No big deal. I'm not hurt. Keach said earlier he's driving to Louisville tonight, so he won't be around to cause trouble."

I didn't mention the boxes Mr. Webb dropped into the moonshine hole, nor his threat. What I told Miss Emily was the truth, though not the whole truth. Looking back, I suppose I should have told her a lot more of the truth than I did. After supper, we went into town. She gave me money to buy a bolt lock for the back door while she left to talk to the sheriff. Together, we changed the lock before we went to bed that night.

The plan to leave with Keach early the next morning now looked like an even better idea for my sake as well as for hers. Before I fell asleep, I wondered if Abraham Lincoln ever struggled with as much uncertainty as I wrestled with that night.

Chapter Twenty-One

Freedom Train

In the darkest hour before dawn, nature holds her breath. Even birds grow silent, as if they are uncertain morning will come again. I climbed out of bed Thursday morning and stuffed what was left of my talent show prize money into my pocket. Mr. Webb missed Grandpa's emergency shoebox when he searched the house. In the dark, I used my flashlight to find the remaining ten-dollar bill and a five. I didn't want to take more of his money than I needed, so I left the sixteen Bicentennial quarters in the bottom of the box. Grandpa believed in a hundred years those quarters would be worth a lot of money. With my mandolin in an old cardboard case, I tiptoed out, closing the door softly to keep from waking Miss Emily.

The lid on our mailbox dangled open in the waning moonlight. I turned on my flashlight and reached over to close the lid. Inside the mailbox, I recognized a page from a *National Geographic* magazine with a picture of thousands of monarch butterflies covering trees somewhere in Mexico. A single sentence had been scrawled across the bottom of the picture. *Buddie, don't go, but if you do, please find your way back home. Love, Adam.* Slowly, I read the words again, lingering over the signature. I folded the picture and tucked the page into my pocket along with my money. Whether I tagged along with Keach to Nashville would depend on the likelihood of Grandpa coming home.

Whistler didn't have much of a train yard. Tracks for switching and reversing engines marked the end of the line for a twice-weekly freight run. The train delivered feed, supplies, and equipment to the farm co-op and carried grain back to Evansville.

"Buddie, this way. Over here." Keach's voice rose from a ditch close to the tracks where she crouched next to Clem.

I slid in beside her.

"First a banjo, now a mandolin!" Clem groaned. "This ain't no picnic. Them things is too clumsy to bring."

"They go where we go." Keach cradled her banjo. "We take care of them, and they'll take care of us."

"I'm only going as far as Evansville to play my mandolin for Grandpa," I told him.

"Didn't you bring extra clothes?" Keach asked, looking me up and down. "Where's your duffel bag?"

"I told you I'm coming back home. I don't need extra clothes."

"Oh, I meant you might want to wear fresh clothes to see Lutie."

"If the two of you are travelin' with me, you better listen up because I'm leaving, and I'm leaving now." Clem spat in the weeds and pointed to an open boxcar twenty feet from the ditch. "When I give the word, run, throw your gear on board, and jump in. I'll be right behind you." Clem stuck his head up like a gopher. After a furtive look both ways, he said, "Go! Go! Now!"

Hearts pounding, legs pumping, we bolted out of the ditch and tossed our instruments and Keach's duffel bag into the boxcar. Face forward, belly down, hearts racing, we vaulted inside.

Clem tossed me his grubby duffel bag and stretched out his palms. “Gimme a hand, gals.”

We each grabbed one of his wrists and hauled him in as wheels clanged, banged, and bolted into motion. A faint chemical stench burned inside my nose. Thin patches of pale dust gleamed in the moonlight on the boxcar floor. Even before we saw abandoned sacks in the corner, Keach and I looked at each other and wrinkled our noses. “Fertilizer!”

“Rats, Clem.” Keach held her nose. “Twenty boxcars and you pick the one that stinks.”

Clem sniffed. “That’s some gratitude. I take the two of you under my wing and teach you the finer points of travelin’, and all you do is gripe. Kids nowadays don’t ’preciate nothin’.” He took a deep breath. “Anyway, this boxcar smells like freedom to me.” He crawled into a corner away from the ripped sacks and curled up around his duffel bag.

The wheels bumped and banged beneath us in a flowing rhythm, making conversation next to impossible. We spent the next couple of hours sitting in a corner away from Clem. After the sun came up, I moved to a patch of warm light next to the open boxcar door and watched hills fade into cropland. Wind from the fields carried the scent of livestock and fresh cut hay. Clusters of houses came into view, and the engineer blew four short blasts on the whistle.

“Clem, what’s happening?” Keach yelled.

“Petersburg. We’re coming into Petersburg. Four short blasts mean the ‘Hoghead’ sees the board.”

“Hoghead? What’s a hoghead? I ain’t riding back here with pigs,” Keach crawled back near Clem.

“Nothing to do with pigs. Shut up and listen. Hoghead is the engineer. The board is the board sticking up next to the track where his orders is posted.”

"Hey, we're stopping," Keach jumped up. "You never said nothin' about stopping before Evansville. What if somebody catches us?"

Clem sat up and burped. "Sit back down. I made this run lots of times. Nobody checks for riders along this stretch. Buddie, crawl on back here out of the light with us. I'll tell you girls about the time I rode brand-new trucks all the way from Detroit to Miami without spending a dime for gas."

I gathered my mandolin and crawled into the corner with them.

"How'd you get new trucks?" Keach asked. "Bet you stole them."

"I did no such thing. One November, snow come flying down. Right there in the Detroit train yard sat a whole load of new trucks—prettiest ones I ever seen, any color you could dream. They was stacked on the car carrier ready to ship south. All of 'em had keys in the ignitions and a bit of gas left in the tanks from the test drives.

"I eased myself into a fancy silver truck and curled up on the seat like a fat possum. After we pulled out of the city, I switched that truck on and ran the heater and radio till the gas run dry. Next, I slipped over into a black truck, then a red one, and a blue. One after another I ran those gas tanks dry until we rolled into warm Florida sunshine." Clem leaned back on his elbows and lifted his face to the ceiling as if basking in the sun.

Keach made clicking noises. "Clem, you're lying. You're lying through your teeth."

"There ya go! I do my best to entertain and get not even a thank ya kindly."

"I believe you, Clem, really, I do." Even if his story wasn't all true, I appreciated his effort.

"You do?" Clem scratched his ribs. "You got class, girl. Real class."

The wheels jerked as the engine picked up speed, bouncing us back and forth. Clem sprawled in the corner and pulled his cap down over his eyes. Within minutes, his snoring matched the rhythm of the wheels.

I crawled back into the patch of light near the open doorway, unfolded Adam's picture of the butterflies, and smoothed the paper across my knees. The mass of fragile wings all gold and orange made me think of the way the sun turned Adam's hair copper in the summer. I wondered if the butterflies wanted to go home as much as I wanted to be back in Whistler.

"What ya got?" Keach asked, peering over my shoulder.

"Nothing." I turned the magazine page over and looked at the other side. "Adam left me a page from a magazine."

"I saw the handwriting. What did he say?"

When I didn't answer, she sat down hard beside me and crossed her legs. "Fine. I don't want to see your picture. What do I care? Adam is only a boy." She put her hands on her knees and leaned close. "I don't want a boyfriend. In Nashville, I'll find a man. Nashville is full of men, and they all play music better than Adam."

"Okay. You can write me all about them."

"Hey, I didn't mean nothin'." Her voice softened. "Adam's a good kid, but you'll do better than him if you stick with me."

A little voice inside my head whispered Adam might have been right. We were breaking the law, and we could get hurt really bad. Running away with Keach, no matter what the reason, only added to my burden over everything else. "Leave me alone." I folded the magazine page and returned it to my pocket.

Keach crawled back into the shadows.

Before long, the boxcars rumbled past warehouses and freight loading docks bordering the tracks on the outskirts of Evansville. The train creaked and crept through intersections where cars waited behind crossing gates.

Clem woke when the train slowed. Holding onto the inside of the boxcar, he stood and motioned for us to do the same. "Most times I toss my gear off when we're 'bout stopped, and then I hop off. This time, I'm gonna protect my stuff." He patted his duffel bag. "I'll wrap myself around this bag, and you girls watch how I jump. Keach, you come next. Throw your bag and banjo on a patch of soft weeds. Spring out as far away from the train as you can. Buddie, you do the same. We'll have two hours here before we catch the train to Nashville."

Clutching his bag to his stomach, Clem squatted, took a deep breath, and sprang like a cricket out the open door. Keach tossed her bundle and banjo and fell into the weeds beside the tracks.

My breath left in a rush when I hit face down in a clump of weeds and sand. I think the smell of wild green onions crushed beneath my cheek kept me conscious. After my breath came back, I sat up. Grandpa would see me with torn jeans and scraped knees. Being wrapped in the stink of fertilizer and green onions added another whole level to the experience. At least my mandolin landed in a soft patch of sand.

We found Clem face down, out cold, on gravel beside the tracks. His cap and bag had fallen in weeds close by.

A yard man ran down the tracks to where we hovered over Clem. "What you girls got here?"

Keach picked up Clem's cap and bag. "Looks like he's hurt."

The man whistled softly at the way Clem's leg bent in a strange angle below the knee. "Don't touch him. I'll have an ambulance here in a few minutes. He hurried off toward the station.

"Let's go, Buddie," Keach sprinted a few steps away. "We have to get out of here."

"I won't run."

"Are you crazy? This is our chance. They'll turn us over to juvenile authorities after they send Clem to the hospital. You'll never see Lutie or Adam again."

After taking three steps in her direction, I stopped. "We can't leave him here like this."

"You're wasting time. We have to go now." She pulled at my arm.

I pushed her hand away. "You've never been right about Wilbur and Claude, about Adam, about taking this train, or anything else," I said, angrier with myself than with Keach.

Three men carrying tattered bundles watched from a distance. Keach ran past them a few yards down the tracks, then she stopped and turned, waiting for me to follow. I didn't move, and when the yardman returned, Keach walked back.

"You girls ride in with this man?" he asked, pointing to Clem.

I struggled to think clearly. "His name is Clem Farney. He helped us ride in from Whistler. My grandpa is here in the hospital. That's where we're headed."

The yardman shook his finger at both of us. "You girls ought to know hopping freights is bad business. You could both be going to the hospital on stretchers and in lots worse shape than your friend here."

"What's going to happen to us?" Keach crossed her arms and raised her chin.

The yardman pushed his cap back and looked at me. "Your grandpa's here in the hospital?"

"Yes, sir, he is."

"You say you know this man and where he's from?"

We both nodded.

"Luck is with you this time. I'll pack you in the ambulance. When you get to the hospital, give them whatever information you know about your friend. Then, go see this grandpa you're telling me about. When you get ready to go home, you sure better find a different way to travel."

The ambulance stopped beside the tracks, and EMTs quickly loaded Clem inside. Keach squeezed in the front, and I sat on an extra seat behind the driver. With sirens blaring, the ambulance covered the distance to the hospital in less than ten minutes.

Chapter Twenty-Two

Finding Grandpa

Inside the emergency room, I handed Clem's cap and bag to Keach, and left her answering questions about Clem at the registration desk. With my mandolin, I took off running down the nearest hallway, though I had no idea how to find Grandpa. The emptiness stretched on until I noticed a wisp of a gray-haired lady in a candy-striped apron pulling an overloaded snack cart out of a room.

"Excuse me," I stepped in front of her, blocking her path. "My grandpa is a patient here. How can I find his room?"

Her eyes moved from my face to my dirty, torn jeans and then back to my face. "Go to the end of this hallway, turn right, and you'll be in the lobby. Ask at the desk."

I hurried on before she said anything else.

The receptionist in the lobby coughed hard before she gave me directions. "He's in room 532. That's on the fifth floor." She took off her glasses and rubbed her eyes. "Young lady, this is a *sanitary* hospital."

"Sorry about the smell." Rather than get in an elevator full of clean people, I made a dash for the stairs.

On the fifth floor, I hurried past the nurses' station and found Grandpa propped up in bed with two pillows behind his head. His eyes were closed, and he didn't move as I entered the room. Morning sunlight streamed through his window, making a pattern of six bright squares across his sheet. A suspended bottle dripped liquid through a tube and into his arm, while a complicated machine hooked to his chest made strange noises.

Finally, he opened his eyes, focused on me and smiled. "I've been waiting for you. I knew you would come."

Half laughing, half crying, I hugged him and hugged him until he pushed me away. "Phew! Did you have a run-in with a skunk?"

"I fell into something unexpected on the way here." That was sort of the truth.

He frowned. "Well, have Emily take you straight home when you leave."

I did not mention Miss Emily wasn't with me. "What about you? When are they letting you out of here?"

"Miss me, do you? Garden's going to pot, I bet." His voice sounded weak and scratchy.

"Nope. I've been pulling weeds. Miss Emily and I eat whatever ripens."

"I knew she'd take care of you." He patted my hand. "We made plans a long time ago in case anything happened to me. She's staying with you? Reckon having another woman to talk to is nice for a change."

"She does most of the talking. I guess that comes from her living alone for so long."

He shifted and looked at my mandolin case. "Are you going to pick a bit for me?"

"Let me tune up first." I closed the door and plucked a couple of strings. We both groaned at the awful sound. The mandolin took a worse beating than I did on the jump from the train. While I tried to make the chords sound right, Grandpa asked, "What about Lincoln's stuff? Any word on the vase? Is everything still safe? I've been wondering how to find folks who understand the true worth of Lincoln's goods."

"No word on the vase. Everything else is back in the trunk including the rifle and the metal box with Lincoln's note." I wished I could have told him the vase was safe in the trunk too. Then I told Grandpa about an idea that came to me for making certain the Lincoln antiques would be properly cared for and valued.

"Brilliant!" He patted my hand. "I think the Lincolns would be pleased."

"I almost forgot. Here's a piece of mail for you."

He took the latest *Reader's Digest* sweepstakes entry I brought with me, opened the envelope, and looked at the numbers. "We've had a lot of fun dreaming about winning. How much has this sweepstakes already been worth?"

"Remember, all the lists we made for stuff we planned to buy? We always laughed about the crazy things we'd do as soon as money flowed faster than water."

"I want to buy seven new shirts," Grandpa said. "One for each day of the week."

"What about a phone? Then I can call Keach and Adam, and I want to call a stranger in Australia. I'll ask about their day, just because I can."

His face grew serious. "Remember when we couldn't pay the electric bill? We planned to leave the power off until our sweepstakes numbers came up. We had hope, and hope makes the dark bearable. In fact, dreaming about this sweepstakes eased a lot of hard times."

"Five million," I said. "We've already won five million dollars' worth of hope from this sweepstakes."

Grandpa pointed to my mandolin. "Speaking of hope, you gonna play a song for me or not?"

I finished tuning my mandolin. Finally, I strummed an in-tune chord and played a few bars of "Will the Circle be Unbroken?"

Grandpa smiled and closed his eyes. Then his eyes flew open as if he had an important thought. "I saw Mary last night. She sat right here on the bed, and she was young and pretty, exactly the way I remember when we first met and—"

"You dreamed you saw Grandma?"

"Dreamed?" He sounded as if the idea surprised him, then shook his head. "I *saw* her."

"What did she say?"

The stubble on his chin quivered. "She said, 'Biscuits are in the oven.'" His face grew calm, and his eyes reflected a deep, peaceful gray.

Not knowing what to make of his news, I played a bit of an old hymn called "How Can I Keep from Singing," in a way that made the strings sigh until a nurse with red hair pulled back in a bun stuck her head in the doorway. "That's pretty music, but we need to take him for some more tests. You can come back in a couple of hours."

I needed to tell him one thing more. Bending close to his face, I kissed his forehead and whispered, "Grandpa, I love you." He'd often told me he loved me, and though I thought those words, I never spoke them out loud.

He looked up with quiet joy in his eyes and with an urgency in his voice, he said, "You have everything I can give you, and you've just given me everything I need." His eyes closed and tears slid down his cheeks. I stayed, smoothing hair back from his forehead until the nurse came back. This time she waited until I left.

Chapter Twenty-Three

Clem's Surprise

The walk back to the emergency room seemed longer and colder than the search for Grandpa, and this gave me time to think. *Why was Clem so anxious to protect his ratty old duffel bag? What did he say about keeping his stuff safe?* I found Keach waiting in the emergency room where she still held her duffel bag and banjo.

"Where's Clem's cap and bag?" I asked.

"His leg is busted." They finished fixing the cast a few minutes ago. They're just now taking him up to a room." She pointed down the hallway as an orderly wheeled Clem on a gurney with his bag and cap tucked on a rack underneath. The orderly stopped in front of the elevator and pushed the button.

I shoved my mandolin toward Keach. "Keep this. I gotta get Clem's bag. Go outside and wait for me."

The elevator doors opened. The orderly rolled Clem inside, and the doors closed before I reached the elevator. The light above the elevator numbers blinked rapidly from one to three and then stopped at four. Soon, the empty elevator returned to the first floor. I stepped in and pressed number four even though I had no idea how to get Clem's bag even if I found his room.

The elevator doors opened on a little hallway between two corridors on the fourth floor. Which way had they taken Clem? Distant voices, probably at a nurses' station between the corridors, came from down the hallway. I peeked around one corner and saw a snack cart being pushed by one of those ladies wearing a red-striped apron over a smock. She opened what appeared to be a closet door and pulled her cart inside.

The sign on the door she entered said Volunteer Lounge. When I gave the door a little tap, it swung open. Inside there were three carts full of snacks. Several vases of half-dead flowers stood on a broad windowsill next to a large sink. Half a dozen pegs held a white smock and a candy-striped apron with a name above each peg. A toilet flushed on the other side of a long partition. The woman who pushed the cart in ahead of me came out of a stall and began washing her hands in one of the sinks.

"Hi, hon," she said. "You're new, aren't you?"

I nodded. "Very new."

"So, this is your first day. I guess they trained you. Remember, don't bother anybody who's sleeping. For the ones you find awake, offer them a book from the rack under the cart. Then, ask if they want a snack or juice. Take hallway 450–470. I've already done the other side."

"Did they bring anybody new up?" I asked, hoping to keep this little charade going without telling too big of a whopper. "I'd like to make sure I make them feel welcome."

She wiped her hands on a towel, then moved toward the door. "Yeah, a broken leg came up a few minutes ago in 458. He's sleeping. I doubt he'll want anything for a while, but you can check. I can't think of anything else. Ask at the station if you need help."

As soon as she left, I took the smock hanging under a sign with the name "Louisa." The smock covered most of my clothes. I washed my face and my arms as far as my elbows then rolled up my jeans and tied the apron around my waist. Thankfully, the smock and apron covered my knees. I might be able to pass for a volunteer long enough to get in and out of Clem's room. Still, the clothes didn't hide the strange odors I had accumulated. Grabbing a can of apple- cinnamon air freshener from the top of a sink, I gave my smock a few good squirts.

The vases of flowers gave me another idea. I dumped dead flowers from all the vases into the wastebasket and added clean water to one vase. A few of the flowers in the wastebasket still had life in them. I fished those out. The fresher flowers made one new arrangement that fit perfectly on a corner of the cart.

I opened the doorway and peeked down the hallway. According to the sign on the wall, I would have to get past the nurses' station to reach Clem's room. That part proved easier than I expected because the nurses and a doctor gathered around a chalkboard to talk. They scarcely looked up as I wheeled past them.

When I reached Clem's room, I stopped at the door and peeked inside. He snored in a deep rumble. Gently, I pushed the cart into his room. When the cart creaked, Clem stirred. I stopped and held my breath. Clem's face, and his leg in a cast were the only things sticking out from under the sheets. I breathed a sigh of relief when he resumed snoring like an elephant.

Quickly, I moved the books from the rack beneath the cart into Clem's closet and loaded his duffel bag onto the empty rack. As an apology for what I was doing, I left my made-up flower arrangement on his bedside table. When I peeked out of the door to see if the coast was clear, a young woman about my height stood at the nurses' station.

"But I'm Louisa," the young woman said, clearly upset.

The nurse asked, "Then who was the girl that went down the hallway with a cart?"

Both looked directly at my face, sticking out of the doorway.

I grabbed Clem's bag and ran in the other direction. When I hit the stairs, a nurse yelled, "Security! Call security!"

At the third-floor landing, I heard footsteps running up toward me. I took off racing down the third-floor hall. The elevator doors opened. I jumped inside and came face-to-face with Keach.

"I'm tired of waiting for you. We have to figure out which train to catch to Nashville. Have you gone completely insane or what?"

"Don't ask," I pressed the first-floor button. A wheelchair leaned against the elevator wall. I opened the wheelchair, shoved Keach into the seat, and piled our instruments across her lap. Clem's bag fit in the carrier behind the chair. I yanked off the apron and smock and stuffed them down between her back and the chair. The elevator slid past the second floor and began slowing for the first.

I slung Keach's bag over my shoulder. "Try to look sick."

The doors opened, and two hospital security guards glanced inside.

"Did a young woman in a smock and apron get on or off while you were in here?"

Keach moaned a little and coughed while I kept my eyes down and shook my head. It seemed to take forever to wheel Keach across the lobby toward the main hospital door.

We were about three feet from the entrance when two guards ran down the stairs. "Stop them!" one yelled, pointing at us.

I grabbed the two bags. Keach clutched our instruments, jumped, and sent the wheelchair spinning in the direction of the guards. We bolted for the door. Outside, we ran until we put a couple of blocks between us and the hospital. After slowing to catch our breath Keach asked, "What now?"

"The only place I'm going is home, and you ought to go back with me."

"Maybe I will, maybe I won't."

"Keach, are you always going to be the stubbornest person on earth? At any rate, we gotta get away from here in case they come after us. Let's go to the bus station and talk there."

We asked a passerby for directions and hurried the five blocks to the station. Inside, we sat on a bench near the doorway in case we had to make a run for it.

"So, are you going home with me or not?"

"I don't want to go back and see Pa. Yesterday afternoon, before he went to Louisville, he came home bruised, dirty, and mad enough to spit nails. He looked like he'd been in a huge fight. I hid in my room and pretended to be asleep."

"He did get in a fight. I'll tell you about that later. What else happened?"

"As soon as he got cleaned up, he drove off. After he left, I unlocked his bedroom door and took some money."

"How much?"

"A little more than a thousand. He had a ton of cash in a tin box on his dresser."

"A thousand dollars! You're walking around with a thousand dollars?"

"Shhhhh! Never mind about the money. He owes me at least that much. I've got enough to get both of us to Nashville. If you let me travel alone and anything happens, you're the one to blame."

"What you decide to do is not my fault."

I walked over to the ticket window, and Keach followed me. The agent asked, "Where to, young lady?"

"A one-way ticket to Whistler, please." I shoved the fifteen dollars I had taken from Grandpa's emergency box that morning across the counter. "Is this enough?"

"Yep, and you're in luck. That bus is boarding in twenty minutes." He gave me the ticket, and two dollars and ten cents in change.

Before Keach could say "Nashville," I pulled her out of line. "Come home with me. You can stay at my house. I can't leave Grandpa or Adam, and you can't go to Nashville alone. If you go, you'll be making the biggest mistake of your life."

"You're trying to trick me into going back. That's not going to work. This is the best chance I'll ever have to get away."

I left her standing by the ticket window and walked to the lunch counter at the far end of the station. When I came back with a large Coke, Keach sat on our bench by the door.

"Half is for you." I set the drink next to her and took a seat on the other end of the bench. "Did you buy a ticket?"

Keach looked at the Coke, grabbed the paper cup, and drank half. "Maybe I did buy a ticket."

"Where to?"

"Wouldn't you like to know?" She stared at the door, refusing to look at me.

I finished the Coke and left her sitting on the bench while I went to the restroom. By the time I cleaned myself up with wet paper towels, the call came to board the bus to Whistler. Keach wasn't anywhere in the station. As soon as I boarded the bus, I spied her sitting alone on a back seat beside a window.

I took the seat next to her and left Clem's bag in the aisle. "You know, you're doing right by coming home. Miss Emily won't let anything happen to you and neither will I. What made you decide to go back?"

She sighed. "You called my bluff. I don't know how to get to the trainyard or which train to catch without Clem. If I take a bus, what would I do when I get there? I'll return the money before Pa comes home. He won't ever know I've been gone. In a few more years, we can go anywhere without people asking nosy questions." She stood, squeezed past me, and grabbed Clem's bag to toss onto the overhead rack.

"Wait! We need to open Clem's bag."

Keach lowered the bag to the floor. I unknotted the dirty drawstring holding the top together. Two magazines with girls in bikinis were the first things I pulled out. Part of the covers had been ripped off revealing pages with advertisements for muscle building programs. Next came three socks, each a different shade of gray, a plastic bottle of pink medicine for upset stomachs, and a faded pair of work jeans.

Keach smirked. "Glad you waited to show me all Clem's valuable stuff. Lucky for us we didn't open this in public."

"Think you're smart, don't you?"

I dug deeper. Two pairs of threadbare undershorts and a shaving kit put us halfway into the bag. Carefully, I lifted a bundle of worn plaid flannel shirts.

"Here, help me unwind his shirts. Watch out. Not so fast."

"Why are you bothering with his shirts?"

"You'll see, if this is what I think it is."

When I pulled away the last pieces of fabric, Abe Lincoln's vase shimmered between us, a deeper crimson than I remembered.

I ran my fingers over the shimmering crimson glass. Exactly as Grandpa predicted, the vase came home when we least expected. "Clem's our thief! I never figured him to be smart enough to plan anything—honest or crooked."

Keach shrugged. "It figures. He knew Mrs. Nelson and probably saw the vase when he cleaned her classroom. He knows how to get in and out of things like locked doors. Clem didn't have to be a genius to steal your vase. I bet traveling from place to place gives him contacts waiting to buy the antiques he steals."

Back in Whistler, we found Miss Emily waiting on the front porch. She knew all about our train ride—Adam told on us. I didn't know whether to be angry or relieved. When Miss Emily saw the vase and heard about Clem, she marched us straight down to the sheriff's office. As soon as we gave him the whole story, he left to question Clem.

While Keach went home to return the money to the box in her father's bedroom, Miss Emily and I sat at Grandpa's kitchen table with the vase between us. I gave her all the details about Lincoln, the cave, and the trunk. She listened without saying a word. Then she said, "I always thought there was more to the story than Lutie told me. So, now we must decide how to do exactly as Lutie and Abraham Lincoln wanted. How will we keep all the Lincoln family goods together and safe?"

I took a deep breath. "Adam's dad leases land for farming. What if we lease everything in the trunk to the Lincoln Boyhood Memorial Foundation? All of Lincoln's treasures will stay together and safe on his boyhood farm."

Miss Emily smiled. "Perfect! I have contacts on the board. I bet they will be happy to help us work out the details."

"I told Grandpa about leasing Lincoln's treasures to the boyhood farm. He really liked my idea too."

Keach knocked on the door a few minutes later. She came in with her duffel bag full of clean clothes. “I left Pa a note saying I planned to spend the night here.”

“Good,” Miss Emily put her hands on her hips. “Now, I have a few words for both of you.” She spent the next twenty minutes chewing out both of us, up one side and down the other. Of course, she had every right to be mad. After she told us exactly what she thought about our little adventure, she never mentioned our train ride again. I came to appreciate the way she always knew how to let go of peoples’ mistakes.

Chapter Twenty-Four

A Storm to Remember

After breakfast the next morning, I sealed Adam's magazine page with the butterflies in an envelope. "Here, Keach. Take this to Adam for me, please."

She studied the envelope. "That's a long walk. I'd have to stay off the road because I don't want to run into Pa."

"The shorter way is to cut through the fields. Please. I need to let him know I'm home. You can keep the album we bought from Miss Emily."

The album clinched the deal. She took the envelope and left.

About an hour or so later, Keach came back with Adam. Between them, they carried three large inner tubes. Adam's smile made the trip home worth more than all Keach's pie-in-the-sky promises about Nashville.

Adam gave me one of the inner tubes. "Keach told me what happened. Dad and I changed the tires on the old truck yesterday. All I could think about was how much fun we'd have tubing down Shannon Creek if you were here."

I ran my hand over the patched inner tube. "This is a perfect day for drifting down the creek."

"That's what I thought too. The weather's been so hot and dry, the water is only a few feet deep. The three of us can go. Dad will pick us up at the bridge about four this afternoon."

The width and depth of Shannon Creek almost make a small river meandering over the countryside. Dry Branch Gulley once drained into the creek. People often spent summer afternoons riding inner tubes down the current as far as the highway bridge.

Adam waited while Keach and I changed into cutoff jeans, old tennis shoes without socks, and dark T-shirts. I scribbled a note for Miss Emily and left the scrap of paper on the kitchen table. Then the three of us walked to Shannon Creek to spend a lazy afternoon on the water.

While we walked a mile or so upstream, Keach told Adam all about Clem, our train ride, and Lincoln's vase in the bag. Now that I had a plan for the artifacts, I thought Grandpa wouldn't mind if I shared the story about the cave and Lincoln's trunk, so I filled in the details.

Adam poked my shoulder. "I can't believe you didn't tell me about Lincoln's cave."

Keach blurted, "Adam, you sure don't have any trouble telling secrets. Miss Emily knew we had left. You told on us."

Adam nodded. "I had to tell. What if you got hurt because I kept my mouth shut? I worried all night. When Dad woke up at six yesterday morning, we talked."

"You were too late," I said. "By then, we were on the train and away from town."

Adam rolled his inner tube down the path. "We called Sheriff Freeman right away, but his wife said he and his brother were out on the lake fishing."

"So, you are a snitch who told for nothing," Keach punched him in the arm.

"No. Dad said I did the right thing speaking up because what I think about myself is worth more than what anybody else thinks about me."

"How did Miss Emily know?"

"We met her at the Attic. She called the police department in Evansville. They checked the train yard, but the yardman from the morning wasn't there. The people they spoke to didn't know about Clem or any girls. The Evansville police were looking for you. That's when Dad and I went home. We tried to take our mind off not finding you by changing the truck tires."

I rolled my tire beside Adam. "You didn't know we decided to come home?"

"We sure didn't until Miss Emily brought you to Sheriff Freeman. When he called us, I stopped praying and thanked God you were both safe."

By then, the three of us reached the fishing dock where we threw the tubes into the water. We flopped down in them, letting our arms and legs dangle over the sides. The current carried Adam and Keach in front of me. I paddled near the bank, leaned back, and closed my eyes against the glare of the sun. My arms and face dried while cool water lapped over my stomach. Now and then, a curious fish darted by, brushing my leg. Small air bubbles rose below the water from around the edges of a patch on my tube.

"Hey! My tube has a small air leak."

Adam and Keach turned around. "So does mine," Adam said. "I bet one or two of the patches on Keach's tube are leaking too. Those little leaks don't matter. We'll reach the bridge before the tubes sink."

As we meandered with the current, wind blew in sticky gusts covering and uncovering the sun with small clouds. Along the creek edge, trees shaded the water, chilling us when we drifted beneath their branches. Birds perched motionless while dragonflies swarmed among cattails rimming narrow places. The lazy heat of the afternoon soaked in, and I almost dozed off.

Halfway to the bridge, the wind picked up, slapping little waves against our legs. Larger clouds scudded across the sky, tossing shadows over us as if they were stray thoughts. I didn't think much about anything until an angry rumble of thunder startled me, and I flipped out of my inner tube. Keach and Adam were both staring over their shoulders past me. Black clouds stacked in layers swiftly rolled in behind us. Wicked fingers of lightning broke beneath angry thunderheads. Pushing my tube in front of me, I caught up with Adam and Keach.

Adam paddled next to me. "We'll never reach the bridge. Let's get out of the water and find shelter."

I squinted at the clouds. "With all that lightning, the woods will be safer than on the water."

By the time we climbed ashore, wind-driven rain pelted us with large, stinging drops. I looked around and realized we weren't far from the gulley and Lincoln's cave. "Follow me. I know a dry place near here."

We banged our inner tubes along as we groped our way between the trees. The rain became a torrent, causing leaves to stick to our skin and clothes. Wind whipped brush against my arms and legs leaving red, stinging welts.

As I led the way along the rim of the gulley, I thought I recognized the hill with Lincoln's cave. In the misty half-light, every outcropping looked the same.

"Lincoln's cave is here in the hillside," I shouted over the storm. After several minutes of yanking and twisting the slippery brush, I still couldn't find the opening.

Adam helped me pull the rain-soaked brush aside. "Are you sure Lincoln's cave is here?"

Maybe ... I think ... I hope so ... The three of us grappled brush, desperate to find the cave.

The ground turned into a spongy mass. Undergrowth choked with water tangled around our ankles. Because we stood on the ridge above the moonshine hole, the cave had to be close.

Adam stumbled away to search a little farther. Finding nothing, he inched his way back. Rain streamed off my hair and into my eyes as great streaks of lightning burst closer to where we huddled. The hair on my neck and arms prickled. In the next instant, a flash and boom disintegrated the top of a nearby maple. Tree limbs crashed into the gulley below, filling the air with the scent of scorched wood.

"What about the moonshine hole?" Adam yelled. "We'd be less likely to get fried."

Chapter Twenty-Five

Death Lurks

We ditched the tubes at the top of the gulley and slid into the muddy trench. The brush-covered trapdoor had been left half ajar. Rain made the wood heavier than usual. With a final heave, we pushed the door aside and scrambled down the ladder. Another flash of lightning split clouds nearby.

Inside, the hole dropped deep enough for us to stand, but felt smaller than when Adam and I peered inside long summers ago. Crude wooden shelves once used for storing jugs of moonshine lined one wall. Now, these shelves held small boxes like the ones I saw Mr. Webb loading into a bag beside the hole the afternoon of the auction.

An old square wooden kitchen table with brown paint peeling and one leg missing sagged against the wall. The light from a small lantern flickered, casting eerie shadows. Next to the table, Saul Webb sat on a broken kitchen chair. His eyes glittered and his hands grasped a nearly empty whiskey bottle.

He looked from the bottle to us, then back in astonishment at the bottle while we shivered near the ladder.

Mr. Webb chuckled. “Look what th’ rain washed down. Tha’ you, Keash?”

"Yeah, Pa." Keach hung her head. "We got caught out here in the storm."

I realized she must have been the one to show her father the moonshine hole.

"Caught me too." A glimmer of recognition crossed Mr. Webb's face. "What you doin' with her? I tol' you to stay away from the McBri' girl."

"Please, Pa, we went tubing down the creek. Adam asked me to go."

"Shut up!" His eyes narrowed and darted back and forth between us. Pushing against the edge of the table, he managed to stand and fumble a switchblade from his pocket. With a twist of his thumb, the blade snapped open. "She's ruining you, Keash. You never pay me no mind 'cause of her. Since yer Ma died, nothin's right no more."

"Nobody wants to hurt Keach or you," Adam said.

Mr. Webb stopped and cocked his head sideways. He leaned forward glaring at Adam. "You one of Jack Gentry's boys?"

Adam nodded while he motioned me back toward the ladder. That's right, Mr. Webb. We're neighbors."

"Got no quarrel wi' you." He pointed the knife squarely at my face. "It's you! You're a big problem. Got to make sure you don't wreck everything." He took one unsteady step forward.

"No, Mr. Webb, Grandpa and I mean you no harm."

A strange gurgle rushed from Mr. Webb's throat. He lurched, flinging the knife through the air. The blade whizzed past, missing my cheek by half an inch, and sticking in the wall behind the ladder. With a thud, Mr. Webb landed face down in the mud. The ladder swayed and the earth around us trembled. Keach scrambled up the ladder. Adam nudged me to follow her, but then I saw him turn back to help Mr. Webb.

I moved to the other side of Mr. Webb, and we each took one of his arms. Adam said, "Get up, Mr. Webb. We've got to get out of here." Together, we managed to help him to his feet. Keach and I climbed out with her pa struggling up the shaky ladder behind us. Adam came last, urging Mr. Webb to keep climbing.

Above ground, thunder and lightning faded, but rain still hit us in swirling sheets. I'd never seen a storm pour so hard in such a short amount of time. Keach and I helped haul Mr. Webb out of the moonshine hole. With relief, I saw Adam jump out behind him. The four of us clawed our way out of the gulley, aiming for the spot where we'd abandoned the inner tubes. The earth shook harder, while a faint hum rose until a roar swelled above the steady pounding of the rain.

We crouched at the top of the gulley and stretched our hands trying to reach Mr. Webb as he struggled toward the rim. A small brown rabbit, fur wet, ears laid back, matched Mr. Webb jump for stride up the bank. The rabbit made a final leap past us and scurried into the brush. Too scared to think, we watched a wall of water twenty feet high bear down the dry creek bed toward Mr. Webb. At the last moment, he grabbed for the exposed roots of a tree along the rim. His mouth opened in a cry we could not hear, and the water swallowed him.

"Gone! Dead!" Above the surging water, Keach's screams brought us to our senses.

I shook her shoulder. "The last we saw, your pa was alive," I said, though I doubted he survived. Keach covered her face with her hands and sobbed.

The patches on all three inner tubes had loosened, leaving them deflated and limp. Adam threw the limp tubes over his shoulders while I pulled Keach to her feet and tried to console her. "Come on. We'll find him downstream."

Chapter Twenty-Six

Lives at Stake

Where the gulley widened and joined Shannon Creek, the flood weakened and flowed around trees along the bank. We picked our way around hundreds of slender broken branches and twigs piled by the floodwaters against the shoreline.

"He's there! He's there!" Keach screamed, pointing to her father trapped in a maple surrounded by floodwaters. Stretched out on a branch where the initial rush of the flood deposited him, her father hung like ragged moss on a rock.

"Do something! Do something!" Keach sobbed while she ran up and down by the water's edge. "Pa, can you hear me?" When the body draped over the branch gave a feeble wave, Keach shouted, "He's alive! Hang on, Pa. We'll get you."

Adam pulled me aside. "Look, he may be alive now, but the way the water's rising, he'll soon be swept away or drown on that branch. Keach doesn't need to be here."

I glanced at her father trapped on the branch. "You mean, we're going to watch him drown?"

"Not if we can save him, but we can't do anything with Keach running around babbling."

The rain slowed enough we saw cars parked on the bridge downstream. People leaned over the rail, gawking at the swirling water.

I grabbed Keach's arm. "Run to the bridge. Get somebody with a boat to head this way. We'll figure out what to do here."

She ran around in circles a couple of times before stumbling off, leaving us to find a way to help her father. By now, the rising water lapped against Mr. Webb's branch.

I'm ashamed to say this, but after all Mr. Webb did to make our lives miserable, for a moment I didn't want to help him. *What if we drown trying to save him? What if he dies anyway?* Both of these were real possibilities. Even as we watched, water licked at the remnants of his boots, causing him to sway gently. He locked his arms tighter around the branch.

Adam walked back from the water's edge and scratched his head. "I'm not seeing any good options here."

Would Lincoln think somebody as awful as Mr. Webb worth saving? I leaned against a tree and thought about Lincoln's words. "Adam, a wise man once wrote, 'People are worth more than things.' Mr. Webb is alive. His life is worth more than whatever else he's done. We can't stand here and watch him die. Grandpa would say whatever we need is right here in front of us."

"We've still got these." Adam gathered our inner tubes. Without a pump, the water will take him before we blow them up."

The rain slowed enough that we clearly heard Mr. Webb moaning. I poked around with my feet in the debris at the water's edge. Then, a thought struck. I grabbed one of the dozens of long, slender branches lodged at the water's edge. "Hey, Adam, what about these branches?"

"That branch isn't long enough to reach him, and we can't swim to him. The current would sweep us past his tree before we pulled him down."

I stuck one of the branches through the hole in the center of an inner tube. "What about using the tubes like rubber bands to hold branches together? Could we make a float? We'll ride the float out to the tree and have him drop across the branches."

"Not bad," Adam picked up a couple of branches. "The hard part will be getting him off the tree and onto the branches. If the water carries us to the bridge, we'll hope Keach has a boat waiting."

We gathered plenty of long thin branches. Then, with a deflated tube around the middle and one at each end, we worked the branches into a tight bundle.

Adam pointed upstream. "We'll have a better shot if we jump in the water back up the gulley and ride the current out to the tree."

We carried the float to where the current poured through a narrow place in the gulley. With each of us holding onto a tube at either end, we slid into the water. I plunged up and under, choked on debris, and nearly lost my grip on the branches.

I wanted to shout, "What if we miss the tree?" Then I realized some things are better left unsaid. With the water rising so fast, we'd have one chance to save Mr. Webb. I tried not to think about bushes and branches hidden beneath the flood—able to pull us under and keep us there until the water dried. The current surged swifter than we judged, spitting us out of the gulley into the creek. The roof of a small shed bouncing downstream with a dazed chicken perched on top nearly hit us.

"Too fast! Too fast! We'll miss him!" I screamed.

Adam kicked down to my end of the branches. Working together, we managed to push the float in line with the tree.

The water now covered the tops of Mr. Webb's boots and most of his arms and legs. He clung to his maple branch with his nose an inch or so above the water. We were close enough to see the dazed look in his eyes, but the current almost swept us past him. Raw patches covered his arms, and his clothes hung in soggy shreds. At the last moment, a twist of current turned our float sideways, and lodged us next to Mr. Webb's branch.

"Mr. Webb, it's me, Buddie. If you can hear me, slide over onto these branches, nice and easy." When he did not respond, I climbed on top of our float and pried at his arms and legs. Adam struggled to hold us steady against the tree. "Adam's here too. Let us help get you to safety."

Finally, Mr. Webb grunted and fell like a sack of grain across the inner tube in the middle. He landed hard, knocking me off the float and underwater. Bobbing up, frantic, I clung to my end of the float. I did not see Adam until, sputtering and coughing, he surfaced, and grabbed the other end of the branches.

Water sloshed over Mr. Webb, but he stayed on the float. "You kids tryin' to kill me?"

He sounded so much like himself, we laughed.

Adam pushed us away from the tree and into the middle of the current. "Hang on. We'll get help down at the bridge."

We let the current take us, though I used all of my strength to kick now and then to avoid debris in the water. Each time Mr. Webb moved, our branches shifted, and he nearly fell off. I tried to hold him steady, but my hands kept slipping. With no strength left, losing my grip on the float meant disappearing underwater with no way to surface.

Sticks broke loose and swirled away Would our flimsy craft break apart before we reached the bridge?

I glanced over at Adam and saw raw fear in his face. Then, he did the bravest thing I think I've ever seen anyone do. When he saw me looking his way, his eyes turned calm and steady. The fear disappeared from his face, and he smiled his sweet, awkward smile. I smiled back. At that moment, sunlight broke through the clouds overhead and gleamed on a familiar VW and a pickup truck parked on the bridge. A motorboat sputtered out from the shore, blocking our path.

As our makeshift float swirled and bobbed with the surging water, Adam's dad, Wilbur, and Claude reached out and hauled Mr. Webb into the boat as if he were a wet mop. When I tried to board the boat, my arms and legs flopped like soggy dishrags. Wilbur tugged on my arms, and I fell in a heap at his feet. Adam climbed in with his dad's help. Claude wrapped each of us in blankets. Keach and a few onlookers cheered from the shore.

We quickly reached dry land. Still clutching my blanket, I climbed out of the boat and collapsed. It took half an hour for an ambulance to arrive and take Mr. Webb for help. By then, he recovered enough to sit up and yell at anybody who came near him. The paramedics wanted to take Adam, Keach, and me to the hospital too. Other than several bruises, we felt fine. Mr. Gentry offered to look after us, and the paramedics left with Mr. Webb.

"Pa's too mean to die," Keach whispered in my ear as they carted him away. She seemed relieved. I had a hard time understanding why she felt anything at all for a father who treated her so poorly. Then again, I suppose a father is a father. How could anyone give one up, no matter what else he turned out to be?

On the way home, we told Adam's dad how we tried to get out of the storm by hiding in the moonshine hole. Mr. Gentry slowed the truck and looked at us. "The Lord must have been looking out for all of you. Lightning can travel underground. The woods might have been safer than the room beneath the gulley."

Keach pulled her blanket around her shoulders. "Sorry. I told Pa about the moonshine hole."

"Never mind about that." My teeth were still chattering. "I'm glad we're all okay."

Miss Emily gave us dry clothes the minute we entered the house. She made plenty of hot chicken soup for supper. The next morning, we slept till nearly noon.

Chapter Twenty-Seven

After the Storm

Late the next day, all of us, including Claude and Wilbur, went to Sheriff Freeman's house. He set a small cardboard box overflowing with jewelry and small antiques on his kitchen table. "When I paid a visit to Clem in Evansville last night, he answered a lot of questions. He said Saul offered to pay him to steal the vase. When Saul tried to pay less than they agreed, Clem kept the vase. Keach, I'm so sorry to give you bad news. After talking to Clem, I got a warrant to search your dad's house. Most of the valuables I found have been reported stolen."

Keach stared at the pile of jewelry. "Pa claimed he bought all of his stuff at auctions." Her shoulders sagged. "When we found the vase, I hoped Clem was the thief all by himself, but I feared Pa might be part of this business too. I figured some of the things Pa did weren't legal, and I dreaded the day he'd get caught."

We crowded around as the sheriff spread several pieces of jewelry on the table. Keach seemed about to cry. I stood next to her and put my arm around her waist.

"We've been looking for this." Claude picked up a silver bracelet crusted with diamonds gleaming in the light.

"We'll drive down to see Clem in the hospital this afternoon. With this bracelet and Clem's testimony, we'll have enough to convince a jury your father is the mastermind behind the ring of thieves. Keach, we're sorry too."

The sheriff nodded. "By the way, I called the hospital this morning. Your father got bruised up pretty bad, but he'll be fine. They'll be releasing him into my custody in a day or two, and I'll take him straight to jail. You won't have to worry about dealing with him."

The sheriff's wife, a plump woman with short, gray, curly hair and wearing a pink flowered dress, came in from the kitchen with a plate of fresh baked oatmeal cookies. Adam, Keach, and I each took three and ate them as we sat together on the sofa.

Miss Emily rocked in the rocking chair by the fireplace. "I talked to the hospital this morning. There still isn't much change in Lutie's condition. His doctor thinks they need a couple of days more to understand what's going on with his heart."

As I munched my cookies, I realized how glad I was Grandpa arranged for Miss Emily to stay with me. The phone rang on the table beside the sheriff's chair. He answered and glanced my way. "Yes, she's here right now." The look on his face and his tone of voice sent an icy chill through the pit of my stomach.

That's when I remembered what Grandpa said about Grandma telling him, "Biscuits are in the oven." His words and the way he'd spoken them stuck in my head, troubling me at odd moments like a splinter in my finger. You see, biscuits are always the last thing to go into the oven because they bake so fast. Telling anybody biscuits are in the oven is as good as calling them to come eat supper. Grandpa always said he would follow Grandma anywhere for her biscuits.

"Buddie," the sheriff put the phone back in the cradle and turned to me, "I'm so sorry. I hate to have to tell you—"

I raised my hand and stopped him. "You don't have to. It's Grandpa?"

The sheriff nodded. That was all.

Miss Emily asked the question I couldn't. "Is he gone?"

"About an hour ago." The sheriff walked over to me, placed a comforting hand on my shoulder and looked at the floor.

I didn't feel surprised. Grandpa tried to tell me he needed to follow Grandma. I understood but not in a way I could put into words.

People began talking all at once. I heard their voices but couldn't understand the words as I stared at the cookie crumbs in my lap. For a few minutes, everyone stood close, hugging Keach and me and saying kind words. I tried to think of the right thing to say, but nothing came to mind. Stray thoughts tumbled through my brain like *Alice in Wonderland* spiraling down the rabbit hole.

The sheriff talked about making arrangements, and Miss Emily made a phone call. Afterward, she sat down next to Keach and said the three of us would be staying together. Keach didn't answer, but curled up in a corner on the sofa, hugged a pillow, and ate cookies.

After the conversation quieted, Adam took my hand. "It's warm in here. Let's go outside."

I followed blindly, not sure of my steps. The storm-washed night air reminded me of the smell of sheets dried on a clothesline. We sat on the porch while stars glistened above like a million unshed tears. I thought crying might help, but tears didn't fall. An invisible fist closed around my heart and clenched tight. If I dared let go, would the entire world fall apart?

Adam took a deep breath. "When I was seven, the tractor turned over on my dad. While they tried to free him, my whole world split into pieces. If that's the way your life seems, hang on. Miss Emily is in there working on plans for you and for Keach. She'll hold life together for now."

I didn't care about the next day or the future. All I could think about was Grandpa. "You know, when I saw him in the hospital, he knew it was time for him to let go of this world." I held my hands with my wide palms and long, skinny fingers up in the moonlight.

"What are you thinking?" Adam asked.

"Grandpa said I have everything he could give me. The only things of value he owned were his hands and his music. My hands and fingers are the same as his." I looked at every crease, bend, and wrinkle on my fingers. "You know what? I'd rather have his hands and music than anything else in the world."

Adam took my hands and rubbed my calloused fingertips. "Because you make something beautiful with your hands, they are beautiful ... like you."

The warmth of a blush crept across my face. Nobody had ever called me beautiful.

The next few days passed in a blur. Keach made sure everybody knew about the funeral arrangements. I used the last of my prize money to buy a new sky-blue shirt for Grandpa to wear in the coffin. I wished I'd bought his shirt much earlier so he could have seen how nice he looked.

A lot of people I didn't know packed our small country church. Anyone who ever bought one of his mandolins or banjos or played music with him came to say goodbye. The busyness kept unbearable thoughts away. I remembered Miss Emily saying, "To God, in fact, all people are alive.'"

That's in the Bible. I still find this verse to be a comforting thought.

The thing I remember most about seeing Grandpa in the coffin wasn't his face. I made the funeral director put his favorite old Stanley chisel in the coffin with him. The last look I had of Grandpa was of his hands, worn out, used up, and crossed over his chisel.

The next Monday was July 4, and the whole town came out to celebrate with a huge picnic on the school grounds. I didn't feel like going, and Miss Emily said she would rather stay with me on my front porch.

Keach went to the celebration and brought barbeque back for us, but I didn't feel hungry.

Adam came over, and the four of us sat on the porch watching fireworks being shot off from the ball field. After the fireworks, we passed around Grandpa's clay pot with the mint plant. Each of us pinched a few mint leaves, and we sat there chewing them in the dark.

Epilogue

Every End Is a New Beginning

Keach never did learn to play the banjo very well. After Grandpa's death, we both lived with Miss Emily in the rooms over her antique shop. When we finished high school, Miss Emily found a job for Keach in an antique shop in St. Louis. Within a year, the manager gave her a raise. A couple of years later, she opened her own shop.

Saul Webb is still in prison and will likely be there the rest of his life. He committed a lot more crimes than the ones we knew about that summer.

Miss Emily and Mr. Dawson helped work out an arrangement with the Lincoln Boyhood Memorial Foundation to lease the Lincoln family's belongings. So, in a way, the Lincoln family's belongings did come home.

After graduation, Adam and I both left Whistler. He went to Purdue where he studied modern agriculture. After graduation, he came home to work on the farm with his dad and brothers. Adam and I still write to each other from time to time. His letters always end with, "Butterfly, don't forget how to find your way home."

Grandpa's dusty stacks of *National Geographic* magazines lured me away from Whistler. All those pictures of faraway lands made me eager to know how other people lived. Leasing the Lincoln family treasures provided money for me to go to Indiana University. Today, I am a music ethnologist which means I get to study music in cultures all over the world.

I'm writing my story while I sit on the porch of a white stucco house with a tin roof in West Africa. A twelve-year-old boy named Waibo is coming up the road toward my porch. He is carrying an *akonting*, a West African instrument similar to a banjo. He says his grandfather made this akonting for him. Every evening after supper, unless it rains, Waibo and I sit on the porch and play music while children laugh and dance. Seeing the joy in their faces is the only pay I get, but a smile on a child's face is worth more than money. People here think I am a strange person from some faraway land, but I know the truth. Most people in the world are poor folk, hoping to make a better future. How we see other people makes all the difference.

Author Notes

Characters and Setting: Buddie, Lutie, Keach, and Adam, as well as all of the other characters in *Ride A Summer Wind* are fictional. Though Spencer County, Indiana, is riddled with caves, no cave with artifacts left by the Lincoln family has ever been discovered.

Abraham Lincoln's Boyhood Home: Descriptions of the cabin and grounds of Lincoln's boyhood home in Spencer County, Indiana, are from the author's observations recorded in the initial stages of restoration (1977).

Bean Blossom Bluegrass Festival: Beginning in 1966, the festival held each June in Bean Blossom, Indiana, is now billed as the longest running Bluegrass festival in the world. In 2016, the festival celebrated its 50th anniversary. Descriptions of the festival Buddie attended are from first-hand observations in 1977.

About the Author

Ann Cavera grew up in a military family. She attended nine schools in twelve years. Along the way she learned good people can be found everywhere. Ann served as a Peace Corps Volunteer in Liberia, West Africa, where she met and married her husband, Jim. Her favorite place to be is in the company of children, often with a plate of fresh-baked cookies. Ann's writing connects readers to the love of God and the beauty of his creation.

www.anncaverawriter@msn.com

E-mail: SpeedingPast80@gmail.com

Podcast: Speeding Past 80 (Apple, Spotify, Podbean)

Made in United States
Orlando, FL
02 December 2024

54882586R00104